Dom's Delights
Copyright©2014 Jimi Goninan
ISBN 978-1-909934-86-3
Cover art and design by Dawné Dominique

Published by
Lydian Press 2014
Find us on the World Wide Web at
www.lydianpress.com

DOM'S DELIGHTS

Jimi Goninan

Lydian Press

*For my beloved Antoine, the best husband
one could ever want.*

ON BENDED KNEE

Dominique's brow creased in concentration as he squeezed the last drops of thick, white cream out of his sac and onto the top. It looked good enough to eat but he resisted the urge, which was a good thing, seeing as he'd been working on these cupcakes all afternoon. He wanted to make sure everything was absolutely flawless and that included having impeccably frosted blue velvet cupcakes – the perfect shade of Tardis blue to appeal to Ben's geeky side. He'd been planning this night for months now. To say he was nervous was an understatement, but he hadn't gone wrong following his heart so far and hoped tonight would be no different.

Being the proud owner of a successful patisserie café was not something you'd expect on first glance at this handsome, thirty-one year old Greek god of a man, with his jet-black hair and striking green eyes. Preferring to remain neatly clipped elsewhere, his only concession to his more hirsute heritage was a rather hairy chest. Truth be told, he was more of a Greek/French hybrid; the French spelling of his name, down to the influence of his mother, was a rather telling clue.

That being said, he much preferred being called Dom, given that hearing his full name tended to remind him of being in trouble as a little boy. He didn't begrudge his French legacy in the slightest, and even appreciated being forced to learn the language as a child – it had proved more than useful when picking up lovers and whispering sweet nothings with his foreign tongue while slowly grinding into their willing asses. Admittedly, he never had much trouble attracting the attention of men and women alike, despite not being interested a great deal by the latter.

Ben had been his best friend since childhood and was now his trusted partner in business and life. His pale skin contrasted wonderfully against Dom's darker hue, and with a silky-smooth, ripped body that belied his geeky accountant exterior, it was hardly surprising that Dom found him irresistible. Then there was his beautifully proportioned bubble butt, which practically begged to be grabbed, licked and generally ravished. Ben was happily versatile but much preferred to bottom if Dom's eight inches of juicy, uncut meat was on offer.

Ben had been a constant companion going through all their firsts together; school, puberty, and mutual masturbation… working their way up from playing with toys to each other. One of Dom's fondest memories was the camping trip where they had finally gone all the way – several times in fact. It was a wonder they hadn't startled the wildlife with all the ruckus they'd made. Of course, they'd both gone on to have numerous flings, fuck buddies and boyfriends over the years, but they had always been there for one another. Especially when they'd both been single.

Their feelings had always been there in the background simmering away, but the timing had never been right. That aside, they often spent a late night together going over the finances, followed by vigorous de-stressing sessions that left them both truly exhausted, but sated. Eventually they'd realized they both wanted to be more than friends, as their encounters had taken on a definite romantic tone… a look across the counter, a lingering gaze in the office. Dom loved every inch of Ben, from his curly brown hair to his big, thick feet and everything in between. It wasn't long after that realization that they'd taken the big step of moving in together; seeing as they already spent so much time together it wasn't too big an adjustment. Dom remembered clearly the moment, about three months earlier, when he'd known he wanted to marry this marvelous man.

Dom had gotten back home from his evening run, sweaty with the heady aroma of masculine exertion, and decided to have a quick shower to freshen up. He slipped off his light blue shorts and stepped into the shower, turning on the taps to let the hot water run all over his toned body and letting it soothe his tired muscles. Grabbing the soap, he began to lather it all over himself, taking care to wash everywhere thoroughly. It wasn't long before he started to get erect – it never took much – and he thought he might as well relieve his tension while he was there.

Suddenly, he felt two hands on his lean hips and jumped a little in fright.

"Don't worry sexy, it's just me." Ben whispered in his ear.

Dom relaxed back against Ben's muscular chest and felt a nice big, semi-hard, cut cock pressing up against his tight ass. Not yet its full seven inches but definitely well on the way.

"Feels like someone's happy to see me." Dom said cheekily.

Ben ran his hands down the front of Dom's body until they reached his dick. With one hand he cupped

Dom's balls as the other playfully stroked the increasingly firm manhood. Ben kissed Dom's neck and shoulders, while he started to grind his cock against his buttocks.

Dom started to moan, his own cock becoming stiff as a rod, as Ben gently started to bite the back of his neck. Suddenly Dom spun around to face him, pushing him up against the shower wall and proceeded to kiss him deeply as the hot water poured all over their writhing bodies.

As they kissed, their hands fervently explored each other; groping, probing and teasing, their precum mixing together between their defined abs into one delicious, sticky mess. Ben spun them around again so it was Dom with his muscular back pressed up against the warm tiles.

Dom moved his hands down, each grabbing a firm cheek, and spread Ben's tight ass wide open. Ben squirmed as the hot water trickled over his sensitive, exposed hole. Slowly Dom worked a finger into the opening, swirling it round and around, as he pushed in deeper and deeper. Ben gasped as the second finger forced itself inside him. He then started to push back onto the hand, moaning even louder as the digits begin to explore his ass with more force.

Dom suddenly withdrew his fingers and could instantly see the disappointment and longing in Ben's eyes. Dom tenderly turned Ben so that he was now facing the shower wall. He then started licking and biting as he slowly worked his way down Ben's defined back, until finally reaching those pert buttocks that just demanded to be invaded. He continued lightly biting and kissing that beautifully smooth ass, getting closer and closer to the center. When he reached the crease he, once again, spread the cheeks apart and began working his way in towards the inviting entrance.

He teased the area, licking around the hole without ever quite touching it, a little closer each time. Eventually, Dom decided to put the poor man out of his exquisite misery and shoved his face deep into the waiting hole and ate like a starved animal.

Ben was in ecstasy as he felt the tongue working hard and probing frantically inside. It was almost enough to make Ben blow there and then, but he was kept just at the edge, feeling his ass being devoured. Just when Ben thought that he couldn't take any more of the teasing tongue, Dom moved his chin into the hole and started rubbing. The stubble scratched along the delicate surface of Ben's hungry hole, with each scrape taking him to an even higher peak of pleasure. Ben loved every second of it, not caring that he was being rubbed red raw.

Eventually, Dom took pity on him and slowly worked his way up Ben's back, sending waves of pleasure all through his body. They could have stayed like this for hours, enjoying the feel of each other's warm, wet skin, but soon other matters became more pressing, as Dom's eager erection slid between the firm ass cheeks in front of him. His cockhead pushed forcefully at the entrance and, using his fingers, Dom stretched the opening further, his cock sliding slowly inside, with his leaking precum certainly helping ease the way. Ben loved the feeling of Dom's bare cock inside his tight, yet welcoming, passage. Neither regretted their decision to forgo condoms only with each other, as it gave them a sense of closeness they didn't want to share with any others.

Ben worked the member with his tight ass, varying between milking it and letting it probe deep inside him. Dom's muscular arms were wrapped firmly around Ben, holding him close, as their bodies worked together as nature intended. Ben could feel Dom picking up a more frenzied pace and groaned louder as Dom pounded harder and faster.

"I'm close." Dom whispered; the slippery sensation of Ben's ass had him ready to burst.

Ben took this as his cue to start wanking furiously to reach the end point at the same time. Their bodies felt made for each other as they built up to a stunning climax. Ben went first, with rope after rope of thick, white cum squirting out and onto the shower wall. Ben arched back against Dom as he came, his ass clenching forcefully around the intruder inside him.

This was all the stimulus Dom needed and he happily began to pump Ben's ass full of his sticky seed. After he was spent, Dom pulled out, then turned Ben around to face him, kissing him lovingly as they slowly sank to the ground. They cuddled together in this position, caressing and kissing each other, as the water and steam kept them in a cozy cocoon of heat. When they felt the water beginning to cool, they helped each other up and out of the shower. Wrapped up in towels they continued kissing, as they couldn't stand not constantly touching each other. Despite their recent ejaculation both cocks were soon hard again, rubbing against each other through the soft, fluffy material.

Dom grabbed Ben by the hand and led him to the bedroom, their towels dropping to the carpet as they went to lie down together on the king-sized bed. He looked deeply into Ben's kind, light-brown eyes as he kissed him passionately. In that moment Dom knew what his future held and began planning to propose right then and there.

Dom had enlisted the help of his counter-hand Sebastian to distract Ben for the day. This gave Dom the chance to close the shop, decorate and provide a suitably cozy ambiance. Happily, Seb had persuaded Ben to accompany him off to his favorite nudist beach, where he was usually one of the star attractions – both on the sand and in the bushes behind the dunes. It was also where he had acquired that delicious all-over tan. It would be fair to say that Seb had easily earned the nickname of town bike, but given how much he'd been ridden he could probably be classified his own public transportation system.

Sometimes Dom wondered how he'd been so lucky to have all his childhood dreams come true – a successful business providing sugary goodness to the masses with a magnificent man by his side. Indeed, at one point it had seemed all but impossible.

He had been interested in cooking for as almost long as he'd been into boys. Dom had spent many a happy afternoon cheerfully baking in the kitchen, whipping up all sorts of mouth-watering creations with his indulgent mother, who was flattered that at least one of her children had shown an interest in her culinary prowess. He adored creams and jams and all manner of delightfully sticky stuff but went to the gym religiously to work off his passions, not to mention all the exercise in the showers afterwards with some of the more friendly pumped-up patrons.

Dom had dreamed of one day selling his creations, away from his father's oppressive rule, in a place where customers could bond over tasty treats and good coffee. Coming from a family of dockworkers it didn't seem as if this would ever be a reality. In fact, when he had eventually told his father of his plans, the old man had had more of a problem with his career choice than with the news, a few years earlier, of where Dom liked to put his cock. Dom had known that if he didn't at least try to make a go of it he would regret it for many years to come.

In the end it was his mother that convinced him to follow his passion. After all, that's why she'd given up a successful modeling career to marry a dockworker, settling down to raise four boisterous boys in the suburbs, following a chance encounter on holiday in the States. She even managed to soothe things over with his father; she'd always been a most persuasive diplomat, particularly in the bedroom. Like mother, like son.

Without any family opposition, all he needed was to get the money for his business. He tried working a series of jobs, but sadly none were particularly lucrative. Things were looking desperate, until he accidentally stumbled across a stellar idea whilst cooking breakfast for Ben, after one of their sex-filled sleep overs.

Dom was preparing pancakes in his small, but well-equipped, kitchen; dressed only in loose boxers that were rather easy to rip down at a moment's notice –

something Ben took advantage of on a regular basis. Ben came in to kiss him good morning when their natural urges took over, one thing lead to another and within minutes both were on the verge of blowing. Not wanting to mess up the floor, Dom decided to be cheeky and cum directly into the pancake batter, with Ben shortly following suit. They cooked them up, reasoning that they loved both the ingredients, so how bad could they be? The pancakes were surprisingly more delectable than they'd hoped, with the slight salty taste bringing out the sweetness of the spreads. After that day it became a regular breakfast treat when they spent the night together. Dom experimented with adding his special sauce into a range of other baked goods and found that the best tasting by far were the muffins.

It was Ben who first came up with the idea of selling them.

"I'm sure the café at ManHole would love to give their patrons an extra protein hit." he'd joked.

"I think they already get enough of a protein injection going there!" smirked Dom.

"I'm serious."

"So am I. Who's gonna want to buy my cum muffins?"

"Well, there's only one way to find out. And you need a better name than that."

Dom knew that it was pointless arguing with Ben, once he'd gotten an idea lodged in that cute head of his, so he relented and called the manager the next day. Fortunately, ManHole was run by Eric, an ex-boyfriend of Dom's with whom he'd managed to remain on friendly terms. Eric was open to the idea and more than eager to sample the goods, having been quite the fan of Dom's product direct from the source. The boys went in the following week, armed with a fresh batch of mini-muffins – a mix of butterscotch, vanilla and caramel.

"Damn that's delicious! So what are they called?" mumbled Eric, between mouthfuls.

"Seed Cakes." said Ben, jumping in before Dom had the time to reply.

"Love it! You've got yourselves a deal."

He shook hands with the boys and placed a small order straight away, before wolfing down the rest of the muffins in quick succession. Eric wanted to test it out on the busier weekend crowd, where there was guaranteed to be many a mouth hankering for a taste of something new.

Dom's doubts proved unfounded, as the "Seed Cakes" were an instant success. In fact, they sold out within the first hour. Word soon spread and the sauna kept increasing their order every week. Dom could barely keep up with the demand, milking many a creamy load to serve those with a hunger for the unusual.

Luckily, Ben was more than ready to help out when supplies were running low, although Dom always took care to taste each load before adding it to the mix. One must be thorough with quality control after all.

Dom soon found that with all the extra money he was earning there was more than enough for a down payment on a shop, and to buy the additional cooking equipment and supplies needed to embark on his endeavor. The only thing left was to find the perfect spot to locate his café.

After scouring the city for weeks, he had begun to lose hope when he noticed that the empty shop next door to his gym had a massive For Sale sign in the window. Not that he was particularly surprised, seeing as it had been vacant for years now. Dialing the number straight away, he got through to a deep-voiced man, Thomas, who offered to meet him for a tour of the premises the next morning.

Before the scheduled time Dom squeezed in a quick workout, to get out his nervous excitement so that he didn't seem too overeager. When he arrived at the shop he was confronted with the sight of a heavenly vision in a suit – a big, blond, Nordic looking god. At six feet tall, the stranger cut an imposing figure in a charcoal-gray, tailored suit. It clung to his muscular arms and legs, and perhaps even more noticeably to a huge bulge in the front of the realtor's pants.

"Thomas?" asked Dom, fervently hoping the answer would be yes.

"Yes and you must be Dom. Good to meet you." replied Thomas.

As they shook hands Dom couldn't help but notice the strong firm handshake, that seemed to last a little longer than strictly necessary and when he looked into those piercing blue eyes he felt a lump start in his throat and end up in his pants.

They went inside to look around but Dom knew immediately it was the place for him. He kept walking around the space but was too excited to be distracted by the strapping specimen of manhood by his side. He also hadn't noticed how closely Thomas had been following him, until a gentle breath on his neck startled him.

"So what do you think?"

"It's perfect!" Dom blurted out before he remembered that he was supposed to be playing it cool.

"To tell the truth we have already had a few offers..."

Dom's disappointment showed straight away.

"...but I'm sure I can put in a good word with the owners if you'd like?" continued Thomas with a wink.

Dom's face broke into a huge smile as Thomas grabbed him by his trim waist and pulled him in close. After some frenzied kissing, and a brief struggle with a belt buckle, Dom was on his knees with Thomas' man-sized manhood firmly in hand. He pulled the foreskin back to reveal a thick head glistening with precum and promptly lapped it up. Dom estimated that he held at least nine inches of juicy cock before him, which he then proceeded to swallow as far down his throat as possible. Years of practice had pretty much eliminated his gag reflex but he still found himself choking a bit as he neared the base. Thomas swore in rapture as Dom corkscrewed up and down, swirling his tongue all along the shaft. Dom used one hand to work the solid cock while the other massaged the full and heavy balls. After enjoying Dom's skilled handiwork for a few minutes the realtor stepped back, pulled Dom to his feet and resumed kissing him deeply; their tongues fervently exploring each other's mouths while locked in a tight embrace.

"My turn." said Thomas, as, with a greedy look in his eyes, he pulled Dom's jeans and briefs down.

Moments later, Dom felt the warm embrace of an experienced mouth devouring his dick. He could feel Thomas' eagerness as he alternated between deep-throating him and coming back up to nibble lightly on his foreskin. Dom ran his fingers through Thomas' soft, blond locks, as his cock received so much pleasant attention. Dom's large balls brushed against Thomas' chin as the realtor buried his face deep into the warm crotch.

The short, black pubes tickled Thomas' nose as he filled his mouth and throat with all that delicious dick. Thomas moved down and took the smooth balls into his mouth one at a time at first, rolling them around with his tongue. Then he gobbled them both up as he wanked Dom, pulling away slightly to stretch out the ball sack, causing Dom to cry out in an appreciative manner.

Sadly, they both knew that they'd have to wrap things up quickly and get on with their respective days. Reluctantly getting to his feet, Thomas kept a hold of Dom's cock and continued jerking. Dom happily reciprocated and it wasn't long before both their loads were splattered on the floor.

"We best clean that up."

"Yeah sauna chic isn't what I was going for," joked Dom, as he grabbed his sweaty gym clothes and mopped up the evidence of their encounter.

They kissed, then pulled up their pants and went their separate ways. That afternoon Thomas rang with the good news that Dom's offer had been accepted and they organized to meet back at the shop later that week to go over the contracts. After signing all the necessary papers they hastily stripped off and sealed the deal with another rousing bout of oral sex. Fortunately, this time was far less rushed and they were able to really savour each other's equipment before once again decorating the floor.

"Feel free to come on by for a free pastry any time you like."

"Oh, I'll definitely be back for a taste, don't you worry."

And so a very friendly arrangement continued for some time to come.

Both Dom and Ben quit their day jobs and threw themselves into the renovations. Thankfully, with the help of reliable contractors, it only took a handful of months before Dom's Delights opened its doors to the hungry hordes. The new business was a little slow at first but they gradually picked up a few regulars. Dom did his best promoting the café, spreading the word amongst his gym friends about their scrumptious range of low fat, high protein muffins. Before too long they had a bevy of buff beauties streaming through the doors on a daily basis. They also decided to keep a small range of the Seed Cakes for sale in the back, for their more discerning clientele – ManHole and the gym unsurprisingly sharing some of the same patrons. It was around this time that they decided to hire a counter-hand to handle the extra trade.

After a brief series of interviews Dom settled on Sebastian – Seb to his friends. A twenty-seven year old blond, blue-eyed, boy next door type…possibly if you lived next door to a particularly depraved den of debauchery. The interview process was sealed when he answered the question of which special skills he had, by swiftly climbing under the table and sucking for all he was worth, expertly working Dom's shaft, savoring each delicious inch with his mouth, tongue and throat. The boy certainly had initiative.

Seb practically dripped sex with a constant mischievous glint in his eyes. His all-over tan was frequently glimpsed whenever he bent over and his low riding pants slipped even further down and threatened to become indecently revealing. No matter whether it was jeans or shorts he always seemed to be nearly bursting out the front and back, due to the bountiful packages contained within. His nine inches of uncut manhood, and round muscular ass, made him much wanted and much had. Naturally lean, he had a swimmer's physique which, coupled with his longer surfer-like locks, complimented his summery look.

He certainly helped draw people in with his easy manner and habit of shamelessly flirting with anyone, regardless of gender, age or sexual persuasion. That, and he was always willing to throw in an extra pastry, along with his number on a napkin, to those more handsome customers that he took a shine to. Dom turned a blind eye to such practices as it encouraged repeat business with many a satisfied customer. Certainly, there were quite a few patrons that had taken advantage of Seb's service with a smile – especially when he had a mouth full of cock.

Needless to say, his trial period didn't last very long at all, as he increased sales and was wonderful eye candy to work with. In all fairness, he didn't just rely upon his looks and was quite the industrious little worker bee. Even that time where the register had broken down and he was reduced to using old-school pen and paper to keep all the purchases straight.

Due to their popularity, they had started offering a delivery service to the nearby businesses and soon needed to add another member to their clan. The winning candidate was Adam, a lanky twenty-two year old, without an ounce of fat to be seen. His shoulder-length red hair, which he usually had pulled back into a cute little ponytail, complimented his pretty, hazel eyes. Not to mention the delightful smattering of freckles over his nose and adorable little dimple that appeared when he smiled. Standing tall, at a bit over six feet, he tended to tower over his new colleagues. Indeed, his height and striking features certainly earned him his fair share of admiring glances.

Adam seemed quite shy on first meeting, but opened up rather quickly. Primarily dealing with deliveries, but also helping out at the counter when the need arose, he quickly proved himself a very capable young man. While they both appreciated his beauty, Dom and Ben felt more of a brotherly affection towards him rather than a pressing need to bed him.

That aside, Adam would have said yes in a heartbeat if either of them had offered. He had even a particularly dirty fantasy about being taken by Dom, Ben and Seb one right after the other… you know what they say about the quiet ones.

Adam and Sebastian soon became the best of friends, from spending so much time alone together in the café. They often played up their closeness for the customers by frequently giving each other hugs and playful gropes, which in turn launched many a masturbatory fantasy amongst the clientele.

* * *

As he put the finishing touches to the main room, Dom thought about the challenges that he'd faced in keeping the business going. Of course, even after the shop had been open for a few months there were one or two kinks to work out, as is the case with most new ventures. One of the first headaches had come in the form of Steve the owner of Sweat Station, the gym next door.

They'd had an antagonistic relationship since they'd met, the main bone of contention being the loss of business the gym's own café had suffered when Dom's Delights had proved such a success with their members.

Steve had something of a reputation for being ruthless and unafraid to abuse his position – as owner of one of the hottest gyms in the city – for his own sadistic satisfaction. Trainers were known to have performed all sorts of acts to keep in his good graces and be allowed to keep training there. Although, truth be told, most of them didn't mind terribly as despite his inner mean-spiritedness, the outside packaging was truly something to behold… and he certainly knew how to give a guy a fucking he wouldn't forget in a hurry.

Steve had a powerful, pumped-up build but had stopped short of the unfortunate stage of bodybuilding where they get so big they waddle when they walk. His short, brown hair, with a distinguished hint of grey at the temples, was the only indicator of his thirty-seven years. Unlike Dom, he was less concerned with body hair and had a good covering of dark hair over his muscular chest, forearms and legs. Not to say he didn't indulge in a spot of manscaping down below; he wasn't a complete savage after all. Besides, he liked to have a clear view when he planted his eight and a half cut inches inside as many fit men as he could get his hands on…and in his position that was a lot.

It all came to a head one evening after Dom had exited the back door of the shop to take out some trash to the alley. He was halfway to the dumpster when he heard a familiar arrogant voice. It was Steve, having a rather animated conversation on his phone. It was clear that Steve was far from happy, but then again Dom couldn't remember ever seeing him smile. The call ended with a stream of obscenities and Steve riled up for a fight. He turned around and saw Dom awkwardly standing there holding the garbage.

"What the fuck are you looking at?"

"Nothing, just cleaning up."

"Don't give me attitude baker boy."

Dom tried to ignore him and just finish his chore without further incident. Steve, however, wasn't going to let it be so easy. Dom dumped the bag and turned to walk away but Steve moved in front of him, blocking his path. Dom's attempts to get around him soon devolved into a shoving match that got progressively more violent. Finally Dom had had enough of being bullied and used his not inconsiderable strength to slam Steve up against the back door of the gym. The tension and heat between the two men was palpable. A spilt second later they had gone from fighting to furiously making out and grasping madly at each other's bodies.

"Umm it kinda stinks here, let's move it inside " said Steve breaking away for air.

They barely got inside the stairwell before Steve ripped down Dom's pants and underwear in one fell swoop, followed closely by his own track pants and jockstrap. They resumed attacking each other's mouths with their tongues. It was amazing how good hate driven sex could feel. Steve removed Dom's t-shirt, spun him roughly around against the wall and then began rubbing his rock hard body – and equally as solid cock – up against him. He spat on his left hand and started to work his fingers into Dom's tight, little hole, while reaching around to place his other hand firmly on Dom's precum soaked dick. Steve wanked Dom as he continued to stretch the sweaty opening. He then squatted down to give Dom's ass a thorough tongue lashing, while rolling on a rubber.

Luckily Steve always carried around protection in his pocket in case of emergency – it was surprising the number of urgent situations that required his attention on a regular basis. Once he had finished priming Dom's ass with his tongue he got to his feet and pressed his purple cockhead right in the center of the wet and eager entrance. Steve rammed his cock into the hilt and started pounding away without giving Dom any time to adjust.

Dom hadn't been fucked so roughly in a long time and was grunting loudly as the pain slowly gave way to pleasure. The sounds of their fierce sex echoed throughout the stairwell as Steve hammered away without mercy. Thanks to the loud thumping music on the gym floor, the exercisers remained oblivious to the hot action happening just a few meters away – although a good many of them would've enjoyed the show immensely.

Steve's singlet clung to his solid torso as sweat dripped from both their muscular frames, the tensions of the last few months finally finding their release. Their fucking was frantic as Steve's rough hands firmly held onto Dom's hips, his cock repeatedly violating the increasingly sore passage. Dom tried to relax his sphincter, while wanking himself, to allow Steve's thick meat to penetrate less painfully but the pounding made it difficult. Each thrust sent an electric shock through his body, but he couldn't deny that it only added to the pleasure as he jerked off.

Steve felt Dom's body tense up and guessed that the *pâtissier* was nearing the point of no return, so he started pummeling the beautiful buttocks even harder.

The fast pace soon had Dom spurting his load onto the wall, pushing back against the brawny bastard behind him. Although it appeared that Steve wasn't ready to finish just yet and kept pumping away. Dom's ass had become extremely sensitive after he'd blown so the feeling of the thick cock continuing to stretch his insides was almost unbearable. Steve pressed Dom in closer against the wall, pinning him in place and leaving him unable to escape the relentless onslaught.

"You can take it!" grunted Steve.

Dom's only reply was a light moaning, the sensation in his ass stopping him from forming a coherent sentence. Steve reached around and took a hold of Dom's rapidly reinflating cock and started tugging at it forcefully. His other hand giving Dom a good couple of slaps across the side of his left buttock, before reaching around and up to tweak Dom's pert, brown nipples. The wanking lessened the pain and Dom forgot about wanting Steve to stop and started pushing his ass back in encouragement. The air was fragrant with the rich scent of man-on-man fucking – an arousing mixture of sweat and fresh cum. Steve's hand, sticky from Dom's previous load, jacked the cock faster, seemingly wanting to bring Dom off a second time.

The big hand on his cock and constant probing of his ass worked their magic and once again Dom's man juice was splashed over the already stained wall. The second orgasm took Dom's breath away, as it was far more intense than the first. Steve roughly pulled out, ripped off the condom and only needed a dozen strokes before creaming Dom's lower back and ass cheeks. Steve pushed in against Dom, holding him strongly as cum slowly ran down their well-developed thighs and dripped to the floor. After a few moments they moved to rest on the stairs, still half-naked with their pants around their ankles, and began to catch their breaths.

"Don't worry about the mess, the cleaners are used to it," said Steve with a wry smile.

In this post carnal glow, they were able to talk calmly to each other for the first time. Finally reaching a compromise whereby Dom would sell his protein muffins in the gym's café and Dom would display posters and flyers for the gym to help encourage the more rotund of his customers towards the benefits of fitness. As an added bonus, the feeling of Steve's rough fucking lasted a few days, giving Dom a pleasant phantom cock reminder of their raunchy encounter.

* * *

Then there had been the time a truck had knocked over a power pole near the café, taking out the electricity for the whole block. Thankfully no one had been hurt but Dom and the boys were forced to come in on their day off and attempt to use all the perishables before they became a rancid mess of slime in the cooler. Fortunately, the stove ran on gas so they were able to use most of the supplies to make more sweet treats for the shop. The four of them stayed for hours cooking and laughing. It also helped that Dom provided a few bottles of wine to help the time pass more pleasantly. After the fifth bottle had been drunk, and the last pastries had been removed from the oven, Dom and Ben went home to sleep, while the other boys graciously offered to stay behind and clean up.

* * *

After their bosses had left, Seb and Adam washed up the dirty dishes and then tidied the kitchen as they roughhoused in their usual fashion – fierce bouts of tickling and mischievously grabbing at each other's crotches. The combination of alcohol and a long day lowered their inhibitions even further and months of flirting finally spilled over into a much more erotically charged situation. One thing lead to another and before too long Adam and Seb were kissing passionately and grasping excitedly at each other's clothes.

"Let's go the office, the couch is really comfy," suggested Seb, having messed around with Ben on it a few times beforehand.

They hurriedly switched rooms, ditching their clothes as they went, desperate to be naked as quickly as possible. Once inside Adam lay down on the couch and pulled Seb down on top of him. Seb started to move down Adam's naked body, stopping to lick the small, light-pink nipples and toned stomach before he reached a tempting, throbbing cock. Seb's mouth started to water with the prospect of eating such a delicious treat.

First, he played with Adam's white, hairless balls, licking and soaking them with his saliva. Slowly he released them and spread Adam's lean legs so he could explore the crease between the leg and crotch with his tongue. Adam's body strained against the couch as the unfamiliar feeling of a guy working this sensitive area with such skill drove him wild.

Seb was happy with the enthusiastic reaction to his work and decided to reward Adam by lapping up all that tasty precum flowing from Adam's eight inch uncut cock. After that first taste Seb was hooked and so he greedily gobbled down all of Adam's manhood, like the true cocksucker he was. He sucked, licked, nibbled and enjoyed every last inch of it, while running his hands over the short red pubes. Adam moaned as his slim sausage went straight down Seb's willing throat.

Not content to be the only one being pleasured Adam maneuvered both their bodies until his face was level with Seb's impressive manhood. He quickly set to work, attempting to repay all of his friend's fine efforts. They happily stayed in a sixty-nine for quite a while, their faces buried firmly in each other's crotches, hands roaming all over the place.

Adam felt Seb's fingers start to prod his tight rosebud, gently at first, but then more vigorously, trying to open him up wide. This almost had Adam shooting his thick wad down Seb's hungry throat right there and then, but he didn't want it to end just yet. Adam pulled back and swiveled around to face Seb again.

"I want you to fuck me."

"Ride there for a ride back?"

"Deal."

Seb flipped Adam on his stomach and shoved his face right between those perky, pale cheeks. Adam loved the feeling of the Seb's hands prying apart his taut young ass, while the talented tongue worked its magic. Responding automatically to the probing, Adam pushed himself back to get violated even deeper. Adam groaned louder as Seb feasted on his hole. It was by far the best rimming he'd ever had and he was torn between wanting Seb's thick cock inside him and just letting the blond hunk continue to devour him.

Seb was having a similar dilemma, as he loved eating a beautiful ass almost as much as he loved pounding one – and Adam's was particularly edible – but it was time to give Adam what he had been longing for since they started.

Thankfully, Seb had learnt a great many things from his time as a boy scout – not just his extensive knowledge of knots and other handy rope skills – and was always prepared for whatever situation arose. In this case that meant having a sizeable stash of condoms in a range of sizes and materials, in a handy little satchel that accompanied him most places. Satisfied that Adam's ass was primed to be taken, Seb slipped an extra-thin, extra-large rubber over his rock-hard rod, applied some lube and positioned himself at the slick opening.

He started pushing gently, moving around slowly in a circular motion, so that the eager hole could adjust to his penetrating cock. He leaned forward and kissed the back of Adam's neck, which made him lift his ass up towards the invading dick. Inch by inch, Seb carefully guided his manhood inside Adam's welcoming passage, taking time to stop every time he felt Adam clench beneath him. Eventually he was balls-deep inside Adam, his trimmed blond pubes rubbing up against the milk-white, soft skin. Seb then lay fully down on top of the delicious delivery boy.

Adam felt the comforting weight of his Seb's body bearing down on him. The initial pain of his stretched

ass had faded and now all he felt was the pleasure of being dominated by Seb.

Taking his time, Seb started moving around, tenderly probing, his movements becoming stronger and deeper as Adam writhed in pleasure beneath him. Seb moved Adam slightly onto his side so they could kiss as they continued fucking. He started long-dicking Adam, pulling almost all the way out before plunging back inside with a powerful deep stroke. Adam was in utter ecstasy each time he felt Seb's cockhead slam into his prostate.

Seb picked up speed, impaling Adam over and over again with quick thrusts. Adam moved his hips back in time to Seb's fast rhythm, the sound of slapping skin filling the office. As much as he loved being at the mercy of such a powerful tool, Adam knew he needed a break – Seb was hardly a small boy after all. He signaled to Seb to stop, who then reluctantly pulled out and peeled off the condom. Adam flipped over, pulled Seb towards him to continue kissing.

After a little while, they moved down onto the carpeted floor with Seb lying on his back and Adam gladly atop him. Adam worked his way down, licking all over Seb's solid chest and tight, toned stomach. He grabbed a thigh in each hand and spread Seb's legs wide. Adam skipped over the cock and went straight to the perineum, kissing and biting the sensitive area, making Seb squirm and moan. His hands moved under Seb's round, tanned ass and lifted it up so he had access to that puckered pink hole. He started softly, by licking around the hole with gentle little jabs of his tongue into the center. This didn't last long as Adam was so turned on by the sweaty, salty taste. He pushed his face in as deep as he could, trying to capture and savour all the musky goodness.

Seb was impressed with Adam's keenness and talent, and couldn't wait to have him properly inside him. Adam was so worked up that his cock was dripping precum. He couldn't wait any longer, so quickly suited up and prepared to slide himself deep inside the wet, velvety passage. Adam took a hold of Seb's ankles, keeping the muscular legs spread wide open and straight. His nestled his cockhead against the moist hole briefly before he pushed. Seb tilted his head back in bliss, as he felt his sphincter stretch to accommodate the intruder. Suddenly, the hole gave way and the cock popped inside and continued until Adam's balls slapped against Seb's sticky skin. Seb cried out in shock but his ass quickly adjusted and he soon had his hands on Adam's ass, trying to pull him deeper inside. Adam built up to a more rapid pace, encouraged by Seb's increasingly loud sounds of enjoyment.

The air became quite steamy with the frantic fucking and their bodies were soon both slick with sweat. Adam's ponytail came loose, his hair falling in his face as he worked Seb's ass like a pro, switching positions and angles to make sure that every last part had been pounded, prodded and pleased.

They continued fucking on and off for hours, up against the wall, over the desk and on the floor, taking quick rests to allow their cocks and holes to recover between rounds. Making quite a dent in Seb's supplies, they tried all manner of positions but their favourite, by far, was lying on their sides, facing each other on the couch. It was like this that they finally both came, Seb emptying his load inside Adam's well-used ass, while Adam blew his seed all over their chests and abs. After they were spent, they lay on the carpeted floor, gently kissing for the longest time. Despite their incredible sexual chemistry they both agreed that it was best they stay friends – albeit with a lot of fucking in the near future.

* * *

By this time Ben and Dom were cuddled up happily in each other's arms, blissfully unaware of the debauchery in the office; not that either would have minded in the slightest. The following day, Dom noticed quite a few sly looks passing between the two young men, but he figured as long as everyone was happy he would not interfere in the recreational activities of his employees. Besides, with the amount of time he spent playing with Ben at the café he was hardly in a position to judge.

However, those slight hiccups paled in comparison to the time they had nearly been closed down completely. It had all started innocently enough one day when Dom was in the kitchen preparing for his weekly cooking lesson with Seb – who had an expressed an interest in taking on more responsibility now that that the business had grown. Dom loved cooking au natural – well apart from a white apron to afford him a little modesty and protect against unfortunate accidental burns. It's never pleasant to feel a burning sensation in one's groin, after all.

Seb had walked in to begin the lesson but the sight of his boss' tempting, firm Mediterranean backside, beautifully framed by the white apron tied above it, made his snug pants feel even more restrictive. He couldn't resist giving Dom a playful slap on the ass.

"Hey you cheeky little shit! Get an apron on and help me out." Dom said with smile.

"That's not what I want to help you with," replied Seb with a wink.

"Later you horny little fucker! I need to get this done first."

"Where's your sense of adventure old man?"

"I'll give you old man!" he said as he grabbed Seb, forced him against the door of the walk-in freezer and kissed him hard.

"Now that's more like it!" gushed Seb as they broke for air.

"That's all you get for now."

Seb was a little disappointed but no doubt took comfort in the fact that he was the reason for the wet spot of precum he could see forming at the front of Dom's apron.

The lesson Dom had planned was teaching Seb how to make the chocolate cake with the gooey, melting center. They had already melted the cooking chocolate and butter together, filling the kitchen with a most delicious sugary smell, and were just about to add it to the mixture of flour, sugar and eggs when Ben came in to ask a question.

Apparently channeling his inner child, Seb flicked some of the chocolate onto Ben's navy-blue tie. Instead of remonstrating him, Ben grabbed the nearest full bowl and tipped the whole runny mixture over Seb's head. Dom swiftly joined in and soon a full-on food fight was in progress. The kitchen was soon covered in mess as they smeared each other with any substance that came to hand. This quickly deteriorated into some friendly wrestling; with various items of clothing coming askew as they their play became a bit more intense. It was at this inopportune moment that the health inspector chose to walk in.

Sadly, contrary to clichéd popular porn belief, the gentleman in question was the far side of sixty, balding and had a substantial paunch.

"What the hell is going on in here?" he shouted indignantly.

"Who the fuck are you? " snapped Seb.

"Richard Daniels your health inspector and judging by this spectacle I should shut you down immediately!"

Although the bulge in his pants did indicate that despite all his protestations at the unnatural mess that he had encountered, he perhaps wasn't quite so disturbed as he claimed.

"Shit you weren't due until next week," lamented Dom.

"Well that's why they call them surprise inspections!"

Dom leaped up before Seb could reply with another insolent comeback and quickly ushered the health inspector out of the kitchen. After a round of begging, agreeing to a series of spot checks and a not insubstantial fine, the café was able to keep its doors open. After he showed the inspector out, Dom securely locked the door and went back to the boys in the kitchen who'd already started to clean up.

They looked at him expectantly as he explained the deal that had been worked out. Seb started to apologize but Dom stopped him short.

"Cheer up, at least now we can earn that fine," he said with a mischievous grin.

Dom ripped off his apron, moved forward and drew them both in close for a passionate three-way kiss, as their hands roamed freely. It wasn't long before Ben's business attire and Seb's jeans and t-shirt ended up in a crumpled pile by Dom's discarded apron.

Dom exchanged a knowing look with Ben and they both forced the counter-hand down onto the floor. He half-heartedly tried to struggle free as his body was attacked with a series of frantic kisses, licks and bites, as they ate away at the remaining chocolate coating his body. It was such beautiful torture that it seemed like Seb might just explode from the pleasure of it all. Dom and Ben then worked their way down to Seb's throbbing cock, which was dripping with mouth-watering precum and making them even stickier.

The boys went to their task with glee, taking turns licking up the delicious juice, swallowing the rigid shaft and sucking the beautiful big balls. They left no part of his groin unloved, and soon the whole area was slick with saliva, precum and sweat.

The boys then focused on his cock, wanking it between their mouths. Seb only lasted a few minutes before blowing his load all over their faces while they continued to worship his cock with their tongues.

When Seb caught his breath, he managed to whisper, "Fuck, that was hot."

After licking the cum of each other's faces, Dom and Ben moved back up and once more indulged in an intense three-way kiss, laying on the floor in a sweaty mass of tangled, toned limbs. Hands were going everywhere, exploring all the sensitive crevices and slippery skin they could find.

To pay them back for their kindness, Seb moved down until he was facing two very hard and succulent cocks. He was practically drooling with desire and quickly went to work pleasuring the boys, alternating from one to the other and using his hands to fondle the one not currently in his mouth. He nibbled on Dom's thick and tasty foreskin while tugging lightly on Ben's full and aching balls. Ben and Dom continued kissing as Seb gave them much pleasure with his eager, experienced mouth. A few times he even tried to swallow both cocks at once, so hungry was he for them.

Seb's skill soon had the boys on the edge of climax, so he worked that little bit harder. He was desperate to be covered in their sticky, salty seed. Their manly bodies suddenly tensed up as they both crossed the brink together. Seb received the loads with delight and tried to lap up as much as he could. By the time they were done Seb's face was drenched with hot cum and he could taste the boys in his mouth and down his throat. Dom and Ben then rubbed the remaining cum into each other's skin as they kissed and cuddled playfully. Seb lay on the floor between the two studs, contently wrapped in a cocoon of muscles and warm skin.

"I want you in me!" he suddenly demanded.

"Me or him?" asked Ben.

"Both of you." said Seb as he quickly fished out some supplies from his satchel.

"Who gets to go first then?"

"Well, it's only polite to let the boss take that honor." said Ben, as he gave Seb's hot little ass a firm squeeze.

Dom moved down and pulled Seb's cheeks apart and shoved his face deep inside them, eating the delicious ass with a passion. Seb pushed back trying to get Dom's tongue further inside. Ben then slid down as well and joined in pleasuring him, by swallowing Seb's speedily hardening cock down to the base. Seb was in absolute heaven with a man on each side devouring him.

They could have gone on like this for hours but they were impatient to fulfil Seb's request. Now that his ass was thoroughly prepared, Dom moved up and started tracing circles on the waiting hole with his thick uncut cock. Seb moaned in anticipation as Ben held the muscular buttocks apart, giving Dom even easier access.

After swiftly sliding on a condom and lubing up his cock, Dom gave a slight push and popped just inside Seb's welcoming hole. He let it rest only shortly before sliding in all the way to the hilt. Thankfully, Seb was so worked up he felt no pain, only the pleasure of being stuffed with hard meat. Seb rode the cock like a champion, letting it probe every last inch of his ass.

Dom grabbed Seb by the hips and moved him to his hands and knees as Ben positioned his crotch in front of Seb's face and put his cock deep down the willing boy's throat. The boys then increased their rhythm, pumping both ends, while Seb grunted his appreciation at being spit-roasted. Dom and Ben kissed passionately over Seb's back as they rammed relentlessly into the counter-hand.

After a good while Dom pulled out and swapped places with Ben. While Ben's cock wasn't as big and fat as Dom's it still managed to hit the spot quite nicely. Seb's muffled moans reverberated through the kitchen as they ploughed him hard. Seb didn't dare touch his cock as he knew that the slightest provocation would see him spurting all over the increasingly sticky floor.

Seb reluctantly pulled off Dom's delicious dick and suggested that he'd like to have both of them inside his well-worked ass. Dom and Ben didn't need to be told twice and quickly rearranged themselves so that they were facing each other, sitting on the floor, with their legs overlapping and their cocks pressed together.

Seb applied more lube to his abused hole, straddled the muscular men, and lowered himself slowly down towards the two waiting cocks. He had to let Dom slide in a little at first as he was too sore to let both cockheads pass through his ring at once. It was an exquisite mix of pleasure and pain as he got closer and closer to the bases. Finally he felt the boys' pubes brushing against his taut, tanned, round ass. He kept still as he let his body adjust to the throbbing intruders. Seb loved being pressed tightly between the two hunks, held firmly in place as Dom gently kissed his back and Ben lightly chewed on his nipples. He had his eyes closed, enjoying the sensation of being so wonderfully stretched, the stiff cocks crammed tightly into every last inch of his poor pounded passage.

Seb started to move his body slowly, lifting slightly up then sinking back down. Each time, he let the dicks slide further in and out of his well-used ass. It wasn't long before Seb was slick with perspiration, his long locks plastered to his head as he continued to ride. Seb was practically gushing precum as he felt their cocks rubbing together inside of him. Dom and Ben decided to help things along by thrusting upward and slamming into Seb as he moved back down. The intensity of the fucking soon had all three of them close to blowing again. Ben grabbed Seb's cock, feeling the precum coat his fingers as he jacked him off. It didn't take much before Seb was ready to climax, his body tensing as he prepared to shoot another load. Ben bit down hard on Seb's nipple, giving him the last little push he needed and his cock erupted all over Ben.

The force of his orgasm made his ass clamp down tightly on the two dicks inside him, causing a chain reaction of ejaculation. Ben and Dom swiftly emptied their balls into the protective sheaves around their cocks, although they probably would have much preferred to deposit their warm seed directly into Seb's ass, letting it slowly mix together inside of him.

The threesome collapsed in a sweaty pile of bodies and lay there for a time just enjoying the feel of each other's bodies resting together. Now, while it was far from their last encounter together it did cement the idea that any future fraternization between staff was only to

take place behind firmly locked doors and out of business hours.

* * *

While Dom was busy at the café setting up the romantic evening, Seb and Ben were enjoying themselves on the beach. Ben, as always, was slathered in cream, to protect his fair, creamy skin from the sun's harsh rays.

Seb, on the other hand, was oiled up and determined to get to an even darker golden, honey-brown tan. After chatting for a bit, Seb was feeling in the need for a spot of more intimate male companionship, so he slipped on his snug, ripped denim shorts and left Ben to his book while he decided to check out the action in the bushes.

"Won't be long".

"Yeah, I'll see you in a few hours, you dirty slut." Ben teased.

"What kind of boy do you think I am?" he replied with mock offence before he sauntered off.

His exit didn't go unnoticed and a few interested beach goers soon followed him into the wooded area behind the dunes. Seb wandered through the wilderness catching the occasional flashes of flesh between the bushes. He hadn't been walking for too long when he came across a couple of good-looking naked twinks, both looked barely legal but definitely not lacking in experience. Indeed, one was on his knees in front of the other and giving a very enthusiastic head job. From what Seb could see of the cock it was very well deserved. They were both quite lean, with a little bit of definition, one with cropped blond hair and the other with slightly longer dark brown hair. Judging by their lack of tans, they didn't spend a lot of time on the beach.

The brunette leaned backed against the solid trunk of the tree behind him as the blond serviced his sizeable cock. Seb was enjoying the show immensely and had already taken his rapidly hardening meat out of his shorts and started stroking. The brunette noticed Seb watching and motioned for him to join in, which he promptly did. He walked over, cock in hand, and started kissing the brunette.

The blond noticed Seb and reached up to take the newcomer's cock in his hand while he continued to work his friend's cock. Seb slipped his hand behind the brunette and squeezed the teenager's firm ass. He moved his fingers in between the cheeks and slid them towards the tight, moist hole. The brunette pushed back to open up his sphincter and let Seb play inside him. Seb didn't need any more encouragement and soon had two fingers inside the young man, rubbing up against his prostate.

The blond had stood up at this point and joined them for a three-way kiss. Seb maneuvered his free hand around and started giving the same treatment to the hot, hairy hole of the handsome blond. The twinks both started moaning louder as Seb expertly fingered their tight teenage asses. The blond wrapped his hands around the three cocks and started jerking them as one, their precum mixing together and coating their cockheads in a delicious, sticky mess.

The brunette took his cue from Seb and let his hands explore the blond's asshole. His fingers joined Seb's in penetrating the blond's increasing relaxed ring. The blond gasped in enjoyment as he felt a fourth digit enter his velvety passage and open him up further. Not wanting to leave Seb out, the brunette moved his other hand between Seb's bronzed buttocks and soon found his target. The entrance was moist with sweat, so it didn't take much prodding before the tips of his fingers were granted access.

They stayed like this for some minutes, fingering, wanking, kissing and rubbing up against each other. Seb decided to give the boys the benefits of his cocksucking prowess, sinking to his knees as the others continued to kiss. He took hold of the brunette's solid six-inch cut cock and the slightly thinner uncut seven-inch cock of the blond and flicked his tongue back and forth between the two. Seb hungrily lapped up the mix of precum and sweat. He then moved his mouth up and down the salty shafts, nibbling and licking while he fondled the two very full ball sacks beneath them. The blond had a light covering of fine hair on his, while the brunette's was as smooth as the rest of his body. Seb wasn't fussy and happily alternated between popping both sets of balls into his mouth, tugging down gently each time. He could feel hands on the back of his head and shoulders pushing him deeper into the twinks' crotches.

As much as he could have stayed there all day, choking down cock and inhaling the manly musk of their groins, he had a desire that needed to be quenched. Seb stood up, spun the brunette up against the tree and pressed up against him. His cock soon found its way between the pale cheeks and started teasing the entrance to the dark, slippery passage. He felt the blond move in behind him and show similar interest in ploughing his ass. Seb quickly bent down and grabbed some rubbers and lubricant from his shorts pocket. He gave the blond one, then ripped open his packet and suited up. Seb squeezed the lube onto his fingers and shoved them roughly into the waiting hole in front of him. The brunette protested briefly but soon began groaning as Seb skillfully coated the entryway. Seb pressed his cockhead against the tight sphincter and pushed. The opening stretched slowly before giving way and letting Seb plunge deep inside. The brunette pressed his lean body back up against Seb's muscular frame, as he tried to adjust to the massive meat inside him.

Soon Seb felt the latex-covered cock of the blond poking around his own hole. He slowly withdrew his cock halfway out of the brunette, tilting his ass back to give the blond easier access. Seb loved being piggy in the middle. How could you not like being balls deep in one sweet ass while another cock filled you in the same pleasurable way? It was the closest thing to paradise he could think of.

Seb took control of the situation, swallowing the blond's cock with his limber ass muscles, and then starting to milk it, slowly sliding in and out of the brunette's tight ass at the same time. He loved the feeling of the sweaty young men either side of him. The three of them were making more and more noise, and started to draw a bit of a crowd. Seb decided to put on a show, grabbed the brunette by his thin hips and started to pound away. The blond soon followed Seb's lead and slammed into the bronzed butt with the same vigor. They fucked hard for a good few minutes but the constant stimulation of his prostate and the tight wet hole he was plugging soon had Seb on the edge. His defined body tensed up, crying out as he reached orgasm and filled the condom with his thick seed. He quickly pulled out of the brunette and hopped off the blond's cock, got to his knees and told the boys that he wanted their juice. The twinks got the message and started wanking their slippery cocks fast, much to the enjoyment of the onlookers.

Seb nibbled at their balls, doing his best to help them to the cross the finish line. The brunette was the first to go, reaching his hard earned release with a heavy grunt. The erotic sight of his friend covering Seb's face and chest with cum drove the blond wild and he soon added his own semen to the mix. Seb loved the feel of their creamy loads raining down on his tanned skin. He caught as much as he could in his mouth and rubbed the rest over his hard body. The boys helped Seb to his feet and thanked him with a series of passionate kisses, loving the taste of each other's cum and their own mixed together.

After the seed had dried, Seb left the twinks to their own devices and hunted around for a bit more action. When he had finally had his fill, he meandered back to the beach to find Ben lazily swimming in the large man-made rock pool. Seb dived into the refreshing water and came up between Ben's legs. They splashed about for a bit, grabbing at each other in a playful manner but Seb refrained from going any further. Not that he minded putting on another very public display but he knew what Dom had planned and he wanted to keep Ben fresh for the evening's festivities.

Later that afternoon, Seb dropped Ben back at the café, after he had texted Dom they were on their way.

* * *

Ben entered through the backdoor and was surprised to see that the lights were all out. It wasn't until he crossed the kitchen and entered the main area that he understood what was going on. The café had been transformed into an intimate candlelit wonderland. Everything had been cleared away, leaving only a small table that had something sitting on top of it. Dom was standing in front of the table, smiling in a most seductive manner, looking devilishly handsome and dressed in a fitted black suit, with a crisp white shirt and royal blue tie. Ben felt quite underdressed in his loose singlet and shorts that he'd worn to the beach.

"What's going on?"

Without saying a word Dom moved forward to give Ben a gentle kiss on the lips before leading him back to the table. As he approached the table Ben saw that it was covered in blue velvet cupcakes arranged to spell out 'Will you marry me?'

Ben was in shock and turned around to see Dom on bended knee with a platinum ring held in his outstretched hand.

"So, what do you say?"

"Yes of course you idiot," gushed Ben before grabbing Dom by the hand and pulling him into a passionate embrace.

"Good thing I've got champagne chilling in the back then." Dom smirked when they finally came up for air. "Back in a sec."

Dom returned quickly and popped open the champagne so they could toast their newfound engaged status. They were both overcome with emotion and their jubilation soon turned to carnal lust. Clothes were rapidly discarded as they decided to consummate their engagement right there and then on the floor. They were buck-naked in a matter of seconds, kissing, grabbing and caressing each other's beautifully masculine bodies.

They devoured one another with the passion of new lovers, each hungry to consume the other in a flurry of limbs and exploring fingers, hands and tongues. Ben dropped to his knees and masterfully swallowed the beautiful cock in front of him straight to the base, making Dom moan loudly. Dom grabbed the back of Ben's head and held tight as the eager mouth knowledgeably worked the shaft and balls. Ben pulled away, took Dom by the hand and dragged him down to the floor. Once there, Ben jumped on Dom, pinning him to the floor and grinding his body against the muscular form beneath him. Dom's hands grabbed a hold of Ben's buttocks, holding him firmly against himself.

They kissed like this for what seemed like hours. Their bodies writhed together, going from frantic kisses to long lingering ones, all the while gazing deeply into each other's eyes.

It was Ben who broke away first, flipping Dom over so that he was face down on the café floor. Ben then shoved his face right between the firm ass cheeks and moistened Dom's waiting hole with his expert mouth. With his cheeks spread, Dom was in sheer bliss as Ben devoured his ass, pushing back to feel more of the talented tongue. Ben moved on to fingering and rimming Dom at the same time, which made the gorgeous Greek squirm in delight and moan noisily.

Ben suddenly sat back and grabbed the bottle of champagne. Before Dom could even ask what he was doing, Ben had shoved the opening of the bottle into the exposed hole, tipping it up and filling the fine ass with cold, bubbly liquid. Dom struggled against Ben at first but as more champagne flowed into him, his body relaxed and he appeared to be quite enjoying the sensation. When Ben had emptied about half a bottle into his lover, he slowly the eased the bottle out and quickly replaced it with his cockhead. He put the bottle to one side and moved forward, kissing and biting

Dom's back until he was lying on top of him. Ben then started to push his manhood into Dom's full, wet passage. The champagne tingled against his cock as he penetrated deeper inside. Soon Ben was in up to the hilt and pumping gently, as his balls lightly slapped against Dom's ass. It was a new experience for both of them but they were enjoying it immensely.

Ben grabbed Dom firmly by the hips, pulled him back onto his knees, and started pounding with passion. Some liquid seeped out and ran between their legs as Ben's thrusts grew stronger. Both boys began moaning in earnest as the intensity of their fucking increased.

Dom felt a little hazy with the bliss of being so capably screwed and the champagne literally being pumped into his system. It was up there as one of the best fucks of his life. Happily, the same went for Ben, who loved seeing Dom's muscular back tense and strain as he ploughed his amazing ass.

Sadly, such pleasure couldn't be sustained forever and Dom felt Ben increase his pace behind him just before he unloaded shot after shot of thick man-cream into him. The throbbing of Ben's cock inside him was more than Dom could take, forcing him to blow all over the tiled floor beneath him without the need to even touch himself. They collapsed back down to the floor, in a hot, sweaty mess. There they lay for a while, happy in the glow of a magnificent fuck, getting their breath back as the sweat slowly dried off of their glistening bodies.

After his cock had softened, Ben gradually removed it from the tight embrace of Dom's ass. He quickly moved down to the opening and proceeded to drink the remaining mixture of champagne and cum, pushing his face in deep to get the last drop. When he was done, Ben cuddled up next to Dom, both of them reveling in the warm afterglow.

Dom's thoughts then drifted from the magnificent man beside him to ideas of spectacular wedding cakes…

BLUE VELVET CUPCAKES

Ingredients:

Cupcakes

3 eggs

2 & 1/2 cups flour

1 & 1/2 cups sugar

1 tablespoon unsweetened cocoa powder

1 teaspoon baking soda

1 teaspoon salt

1 & 1/4 cups vegetable oil

1 cup milk

1 teaspoon lemon juice

1 tablespoons dark blue food coloring

1 teaspoon violet food coloring

1 teaspoon vanilla extract

Icing

4 cups icing sugar

1 cup Crisco

3 tablespoons water

1 teaspoon vanilla extract

Instructions:

Preheat oven to 180°C (350°F)

Line cupcake pans with paper liners or use a silicon cupcake mould.

Mix together the flour, sugar, cocoa powder, baking soda, and salt in a large bowl.

In another large bowl, mix the eggs, oil, milk, food coloring, vanilla and lemon juice.

Whisk until smooth and well combined.

Add the contents of the first bowl to the second and mix until smooth again.

Pour the mixture into the liners or mould, only filling until 2/3 full.

Bake for 18-20 minutes. To test if they are cooked, insert a toothpick in the center and if it comes out clean then they are ready.

While cupcakes are cooking, combine all the ingredients for the icing into a bowl. Best to use an electric mixer for faster results.

Take the cupcakes out of the oven and leave to cool before decorating with the icing.

BUTTERSCOTCH SEED CAKES

Ingredients:

2 eggs

3 cups flour

1 cup sugar

1/2 cup butter

1 cup milk

1 teaspoon lemon juice

4 teaspoons baking powder

1 teaspoon salt

1 teaspoon ground cinnamon

3/4 teaspoon vanilla extract

1 cup butterscotch chips

As much fresh man cream as you desire.

Instructions:

Preheat oven to 180°C (350°F)

Lay muffin cups on a tray or use a silicon mould.

Mix together the flour, baking powder, cinnamon and salt in a large bowl.

In another large bowl, mix the eggs, milk, lemon juice, butter and vanilla extract together.

Add the two bowls together, mixing well before adding the butterscotch chips.

Continue mixing until the chips are fairly evenly distributed.

Add the desired amount of fresh man cream and mix well.

Pour the mixture into the cups or mould, only filling until 2/3 full.

Bake for 25-30 minutes or until golden brown.

FONDANT CHOCOLATE CAKE

Ingredients:

5 eggs

3/4 cup flour

1 & 1/3 cups sugar

3/4 cups butter

1 & 3/4 cups dark melting chocolate

Instructions:

Preheat oven to 180°C (350°F)

Melt the chocolate and the butter together in a saucepan.

Whisk the eggs and sugar together in another bowl.

Add the flour.

Mix well.

Add the chocolate and butter and mix well again.

Put into a greased cake pan.

Bake in the oven for 15 minutes.

Leave on the counter for 5-10 minutes to cool slightly before serving.

BACHELOR PARTY BLOWOUT

Beads of sweat ran down Dom's broad, bare back, as his warm hands moved at a frantic pace, getting stickier by the moment, but he was determined to get his sweet reward.

The young *pâtissier* was hard at work at his café – naked, bar his tight, white apron – busily trying out different cake recipes ahead of his fast approaching wedding. They'd settled on a date for early summer, figuring it would give them almost a year to plan their perfect day, but it still seemed like the days were flying by at an alarming rate. Their lives hadn't been exactly quiet of late, what with organizing the wedding and searching for a new apartment they barely had enough time to choose centerpieces, let alone fuck – not to say Dom didn't hungrily jump on Ben whenever the opportunity arose.

It wasn't an unusual occurrence for him to be cooking in this manner; indeed his staff quite enjoyed the view when popping into the kitchen to grab something or other for the café. At present, he was in the middle of making a White Chocolate Vanilla Speculoos Cheesecake. The kitchen was like a sauna and the perspiration was dripping down off of his meaty, masculine form as he stirred the sticky mixture with his favorite wooden spoon.

Ben was passing by the door when he spied his fiancé's firm, muscular ass being beautifully framed by the apron and couldn't resist the temptation for a closer inspection. He dropped to his knees and stared at it, salivating, before leaning in to show his appreciation.

Dom was so engrossed in his task he didn't hear Ben come in and only became aware that he had company when he felt two masculine hands spread his ass cheeks, followed by a tongue starting to gently probe inside. Dom wasn't too startled as this wasn't the first time, and no doubt wouldn't be the last, that he'd been interrupted this way.

As he ate with increasing passion, Ben unbuttoned his sky-blue business shirt, exposing his defined abs and chest. Dom pushed back allowing Ben to work his face deeper into the moist, warm hole. Ben reached around under the apron until he found Dom's increasingly hard

erection, rubbing his fingers over the cockhead, which was slick with precum. Dom moaned louder as Ben continued to eat his ass with gusto while lightly stroking Dom's cock. Ben kept on happily eating this manly treat, enjoying the sounds of pleasure emanating from his beau.

As much as Dom appreciated the attention he wanted more. He spun around and pulled Ben to his feet, kissing him deeply as he undid Ben's black trousers and freed that delightful dick from its confining wrapping. They kept kissing as Ben's trousers and underwear fell to his ankles and Dom cast his apron to the side. Dom's hands moved all over the smooth skin of Ben's deliciously defined back and buttocks. They slowly sank down to the floor, rolling around together on the white tiles. Ben kicked off his shoes and trousers so that they were completely naked, wrapped up together in a hot, loving embrace; their sweaty, muscular bodies writhing together in pleasure as they made love on the kitchen floor. Dom maneuvered around so that they had their faces in each other's crotches and the cocksucking really began in earnest. Despite their many years together, the passion between them was just as strong as it had been when they were teenagers having a sneaky shag during one of their many sleepovers…the garden shed in Dom's backyard in particular had been one of their favorite secret spots to play.

After a good ten minutes of mutual fellatio, Dom decided he'd much rather Ben be fucking his ass instead of his mouth. He stood up, helped Ben to his feet, and grabbed a handful of white chocolate cake mixture from the bowl, making sure that he thoroughly coated Ben's manhood and his own hungry hole with the gooey concoction.

Ben took the hint and swiftly put his cockhead at the sticky white entrance as Dom bent over the stainless steel counter. They had used all sorts of foodstuffs for lubrication in the past – butter, cooking oil, Crisco…but chocolate was definitely a first. It proved surprisingly effective as Ben slid his full seven inches inside the tight passage with no great resistance and was soon pounding Dom with gay abandon. Ben bent over and kissed the back of Dom's neck as he continued working his cock in and out, the chocolaty mixture running down their strong, shapely legs.

It was at this opportune time that Seb, their counter-hand, walked into the kitchen, as he was preparing to open Dom's Delights for the morning rush. He stopped, mid-step, transfixed by the sight of Ben's toned, white ass contracting with each thrust as he pumped into Dom. Seb wasted no time – he pulled his own rapidly hardening cock from his tight, low-riding denim shorts and wanked lazily while enjoying the show.

Dom and Ben were oblivious to their audience, not that either of them would have minded terribly, as Seb had already been their ready playmate on more than a few occasions.

Ben pulled out and moved Dom down to the floor onto his hands and knees. As he turned Ben caught sight of Seb wanking in the doorway but decided to pretend he hadn't and simply continued on with the show. Once in position he started pounding away with greater force as Dom uttered encouragement between grunts of pleasure.

Seb loved the sight of his bosses fornicating – Ben's pale, athletic build colliding against Dom's darker Greek, god-like form. Their fucking built up to a frantic pace as Ben repeatedly slammed into Dom.

Ben passionately pounded away until he couldn't hold off anymore and unloaded deep inside Dom's ass. After he was completely spent Ben pulled out his cock - all white with chocolate and cum – and looked over his shoulder at Seb.

"Wanna taste?" Ben asked with a mischievous grin.

Seb didn't need a second invitation and joined them as fast as he could, giving a quick lick to Ben's still erect cock before shoving his face straight into Dom's well-used hole.

Dom was confused as to who Ben was talking to but soon guessed the identity of their guest when he felt the familiar tongue exploring, so he pushed back and enjoyed the erotic sensation of Seb lapping up all the delicious chocolate-cum goodness. Ben moved around in front of Dom and lovingly kissed him before gently guiding his fiancé's head down to his cock, so that Dom could eat up the remaining mixture.

Dom loved having his ass eaten while Ben's thick cock slid in and out of his mouth getting cleaner and cleaner as the chocolate came away and went down his throat.

Eating his boss's hot hole had given Seb an appetite for something else, so he reached into his pocket and grabbed a condom. As a former boy scout, he was always well prepared for whatever arose and when you were a bronzed surfer boy with a nine-inch cock and beautiful round ass it really wasn't surprising how often things came up. He slid the rubber on and slammed himself into Dom's inviting passage. Seb didn't bother asking because he knew Dom well enough to know that he rarely refused the offer of a nice, big, hard cock roughly probing his insides.

He was correct, and after a little period of adjustment – Seb being a few inches bigger than Ben – Dom was pushing back into Seb's crotch trying to get him in as deep as possible, all the while greedily chowing down on Ben's succulent, cut cock.

Dom was happy being spit-roasted but knew they had to wrap things up shortly so they could open the café and serve their patiently waiting customers. He pointed at the big clock on the far wall and his companions realized their playtime was headed towards a swift, albeit happy, ending.

Luckily, after getting all worked up watching the boys fucking, Seb was in need of quick relief and gave Dom a fast and furious pounding that filled the kitchen with the sound of sweaty skin slapping together and the lustful moans of men. Soon Seb was filling his condom with a hot load just as Ben had worked up a second shot to deposit directly down Dom's throat.

When they were done, Seb and Ben both withdrew and flipped Dom over to help him get his final release. Seb worked the big balls with his mouth, expertly fingering his grateful boss while Ben deep-throated the thick, uncut piece of Greek meat. It didn't take long before Dom's seed was filling Ben's mouth and throat with a little dripping out his mouth and back down his pulsing cock, which Seb eagerly licked up.

"OK fun's over, time to get to work." said Dom. They laughed and lay there for a bit longer just enjoying the feel of each other's naked bodies, resting together before cleaning up and putting on their clothes.

* * *

Dom and Ben's love story wasn't the only one connected to the happy family at the café, although the second pairing came as quite the surprise. The retiring delivery boy, Adam, was seemingly the most unlikely match for Steve, the gruff gym owner next door.

The first time Adam saw Steve his pants tightened and his heart quickened. He was dropping off the first lot of protein muffins to the gym, after Steve and Dom had reached their mutually satisfying accord the previous week – in a bout of frenzied fucking in the stairwell behind the gym. It was 5.30 in the morning and Steve was only wearing a skimpy pair of red workout shorts, which were moist with exertion and clung to his sizeable package. Steve liked to do his workout before anyone else arrived, so that his hairy body was pumped-up with his skin taut over his bulging muscles. Adam found himself all flustered and could barely get out the words that he was there for the delivery.

Steve was his perfect fantasy, just standing there in the flesh. Adam loved to play with older, more muscular, guys which, despite being a stereotypical indication of daddy issues, couldn't be further from the truth. In fact, he had a wonderful relationship with his own father.

Steve had caught glimpses of the delivery boy before but hadn't really paid much attention seeing he wasn't normally drawn to twinks. Besides he had never wanted to be accused of robbing the cradle – nothing sadder than appearing to be chasing after one's lost youth, after all. That being said, there was something about the shy, stammering and rather adorable boy, that, while giving him a familiar feeling in his groin also came with a curious new sensation that he couldn't quite put his finger on – although he certainly hadn't had any problems knowing where to stick his fingers in the past.

Steve told Adam to put the muffins in the kitchen and followed in closely behind him. Adam didn't realize this and after quickly placing the order on the counter he spun around, ran straight into the hard wall of muscle that was Steve and nearly fell backwards. Steve instinctively caught and held him in a tight grasp. Adam started to splutter out an apology but was quickly silenced with a passionate kiss. Normally for Steve this is where it would have turned into a quickie in the kitchen.

Adam, however, while enjoying the kiss immensely, had a sudden crisis of confidence and broke contact, rushing away as fast as his lithe legs could carry him.

"See you tomorrow?" Steve called out to Adam's retreating form.

Steve was confused, frustrated and altogether intrigued as he was far from used to anyone refusing him. Fortunately, he had relief later that day when he was called to deal with a report of inappropriate behavior in the steam room. Not that he minded what the guys got up to but sometimes a member would get put out by the shenanigans of others – especially if they weren't being included. Steve had walked in the shower area to find two guys he recognized as regulars in the middle of a rather enthusiastic embrace. His first thought had been to stop them but his encounter with Adam had left him riled up. So, he had grabbed both men roughly by the arms and pulled them into the nearest toilet cubicle and thoroughly reprimanded them with his cock. Needless to say it wasn't much of a deterrent, but everyone got what they deserved.

Adam was more cautious the next few mornings, and Steve played the part of the perfect gentleman, with neither of them mentioning the incident. The gym owner was trying hard to reconcile this foreign sensation of feeling protective as well as predatory towards the sweet-faced, yet thoroughly tempting, delivery boy. After a week they started chatting; at first just innocent comments about the weather but gradually building up to more personal subjects, such as plans for the weekend. This was completely new territory for Steve as he felt a strange desire to actually get to know this lad as opposed to the many men he had simply treated as useful bits of meat.

As the weeks went by, Adam developed more self-assurance around Steve and decided he should make the next move. One morning he arrived in his tightest t-shirt and jeans that cradled his assets sublimely. He walked in, set down the box, marched straight up to Steve and kissed him in a most passionate fashion, before breaking away.

Steve, while somewhat startled, promptly responded in kind, pushing Adam back up against the front counter at reception and eagerly violated the young man's mouth with his tongue in return. Adam enjoyed this for a few minutes before forcefully pushing Steve back.

"If you want more you're going to have to take me out."

"Pick you up Friday night at 7?"

"Dinner and a movie?"

"Done!"

The date was a smashing success and they had barely finished their mains before forgetting about the movie, skipping desert and racing back to Steve's apartment to fervently consummate a few months worth of mutual lust and longing.

After an initial burst of furious making out and groping they slowed down and started kissing gently. This was a new experience for Steve, as he wasn't used to softness in his sexual encounters. He had gone from early teen fumbles in locker rooms and cramped back seats into the more frenzied, fast sessions with anonymous guys in sauna cabins. He had had a string of early, half-hearted relationships in his twenties but his constant desire for fresh cock usually drove them apart. He didn't know what it was about Adam that drew out this gentler side of him but he wasn't opposed to it.

The tenderness soon gave way to unbridled passion. Clothes were quickly discarded and Steve easily hoisted Adam up so that his legs were wrapped around his waist and carried him into the bedroom. Throwing Adam down on the bed, Steve jumped on top of him, covering Adam's lean form with his own muscular build. They rolled around for hours exploring each other's bodies, taking the time to discover all the sensitive spots and pleasure each other fully. Steve was soon a great fan of the delivery boy's smooth, lean body. He took much pleasure in finding and kissing all the little freckles spread about Adam's pale skin.

Adam in turn loved Steve's body hair, running his fingers, then his tongue, all through the more hirsute areas, especially the armpits and ass crack. The latter soon had all of his attention as he thrust his face as deep inside Steve's thoroughly enticing entrance as humanly possible. Adam was far from the innocent that he appeared to be.

Normally, Steve wasn't that interested in being rimmed but Adam was doing such a spectacular job he felt no desire to stop him feasting on his ass. Steve was very much impressed with Adam's skill and even found himself pushing back against the apparently very, hungry mouth.

From here they happily and hungrily moved on to each other's cocks, giving each of them just as much eager attention. Their sweaty bodies stayed tightly wrapped up together, as their movements varied between fierce and frenzied through to more gentle and loving. At this point Steve would have usually taken control and just ploughed Adam's hot, white ass without a second thought, but the whole encounter had thrown him out of his comfort zone and had him keen to try something new. So, in a move that was completely out of character, and rather shocking to Steve himself, he offered to bottom. Indeed, everyone – Steve included – would have said the possibility of Britney singing live was a far more likely option than his ever willingly taking on a passive role.

Adam was surprised but gladly accepted the generous offer. Steve stressed that Adam really had to go slow and use lots of lubrication. Not that this was a kindness he had shown to the many others who'd asked the same of him, mind you. Granted, Steve's conquests tended not to complain once the pain of the rough fucking had faded into far more pleasant sensations.

Steve was far less experienced than he'd ever admit to. Truth be told, the only action his ass had seen was the occasional dildo after a drunken night out when he needed to scratch a certain itch. It wasn't that he was against being fucked per se, it was more that he didn't like the loss of control.

Adam realized that Steve was showing an unexpected vulnerability and found that he liked him even more for it. He was coming to understand that there was far more to this solid muscleman than just his gruff exterior.

Steve generously applied lube to himself and Adam's condom-covered cock before rolling onto his back, spreading his legs wide and waiting for Adam to penetrate him. Adam took his position at the entrance, supporting Steve's thick, muscular legs up against his body. They locked eyes as Adam slowly pushed himself inside Steve's hairy hole. Although he had started softly, Steve's groans of pleasure soon had him furiously pounding away. Adam loved the feel of driving his manhood into Steve's virginal-like ass. Neither of them lasted particularly long as the experience was incredibly intense and had them blowing within moments of one another. Adam collapsed down onto Steve's burly chest, leaving his cock inside the warm passage. They started kissing and soon were rock-hard again and eager for round two. There were many rounds that night, with much flip-flopping – versatility being a much-valued virtue – until both were rather sore but smilingly sated.

There was no second date as they basically jumped headlong into a relationship. Their fucking always tended more towards lovemaking and was more intense than Steve had ever known or thought he'd wanted – although this was hardly surprising given how smitten he was with the boy.

Steve became a lot friendlier to those around him with many staff members and gym-goers noticing the change for the better. Of course, the new couple was subject to the occasional biblical joke about snakes and eating each other's forbidden fruits but it was all in good humor.

Their inability to keep their hands to themselves, as is the case with most budding relationships, meant that Adam's morning deliveries had started taking longer and longer. Not that Dom minded; he much preferred this kinder version of Steve to the angry mountain of muscle he had been used to dealing with – not to say he hadn't enjoyed the electrically violent sex they'd shared in that dirty stairwell a few months previously.

***

There was still much to do before the big day – choosing rings and suits, settling on a venue, finalizing the guest list and deciding who to ask to be their best men. Well, the last was perhaps the easiest task of all, and after a very short discussion they realized that they were agreed upon who they wanted to be by their sides. The following weekend they took Seb and Adam out to dinner in one of the city's finest eateries to ask them if they'd like to take on the roles. Both boys were honored and happily accepted without a moment's hesitation, immediately offering to lend a helping hand with the arrangements, where possible, to lighten their loads.

Even with all their assistance, Dom knew that he would have to hire extra staff to help out beforehand and to cover while they were away on their honeymoon. He promptly placed an ad in the paper and soon had a whole host of resumes on his desk. His first concern was the hiring of another *pâtissier* to help out with the cooking. It was important that the new hire could not only cook well but that they were also a good fit for their happy work family. Dom wasn't a fan of formal interviews, so he encouraged the candidates to come in fairly casual attire to aid in keeping the mood light. After interviewing quite a few people, Dom still hadn't found the right applicant. They all looked good on paper but each time there was a certain something lacking.

Then on the third day of interviews in walked Andy, a rather handsome young man with skin the color of mocha that you just wanted to lick. Not to mention a gym-fit body that filled out his jeans and dark green t-shirt quite nicely. It wasn't his looks that struck Dom straight away, although they weren't easy to miss, it was his soothingly relaxed manner that immediately put you at ease. It wasn't long into the interview that Dom knew that he had found the perfect person to join their tight-knit crew. If that wasn't enough, Andy had brought in a Key Lime Pie, which was to die for – especially to anyone who found about the calorie count afterwards. Frankly, the pie in itself would have been enough to seal the deal and indeed soon became a definite customer favorite – as did he.

As soon as Seb met Andy he knew he had to have him – preferably naked and pressing down on top of him. So he set to work straight away with a campaign of forceful flirting and quite a lot of "accidental" brushing up against the new *pâtissier*.

Andy found all the attention rather flattering and, truth be told, had quite the penchant for blonds but thought he'd make Seb work a little for it seeing he'd heard about the counter-hand's reputation for getting everything he set his cock after.

After about two tortuous weeks Andy decided to give Seb what he so desperately craved. As they were putting away stock into the walk-in freezer, Andy came up behind Seb, grabbed him by the waist and pulled him close. He started wildly biting the nape of his neck causing Seb to arch his back and push his fuckable, round ass up against the handsome man behind him. Their nipples were popping through their light t-shirts, as the cold and sexual arousal took effect.

Seb could feel Andy's cock steadily growing in his pants and poking into the back of Seb's jeans.

"About time." Seb whispered.

"Hush up," replied Andy as he spun Seb around and planted a fiery kiss on his open mouth.

Andy's lips were just as soft and luscious as Seb had imagined them to be. Their kissing grew in intensity as their hands explored each other through their clothes, heating them up despite the chilly temperature of the freezer.

Andy pushed Seb back against the rack full of ice cream, swiftly dropped to his knees on the cold, hard floor and had Seb's jeans unbuckled in a flash. Not wasting any time, he quickly swallowed Seb's thick, juicy cock in one gulp.

Seb cried out in pleasure and grabbed the back of Andy's head as he felt a frosty nose nuzzling against his pubes. There weren't many men that could take Seb in one go and he was impressed by Andy's abilities. He let Andy corkscrew up and down on his cock, as he leaned up against the icy shelves, his ass cheeks cupped by Andy's large, solid and reassuringly strong hands.

They soon switched positions, as Seb was ravenous for Andy's thick meat. Andy's cock was slightly bigger than Seb's nine inches but he valiantly worked his way down the base, gagging a few times on the way but persisting until he felt Andy's full, black balls rubbing against his chin. He enthusiastically worked the shaft with his tongue and milked the cock for all he was worth.

Andy's moans became louder and louder as he came closer to the edge.

"Careful I'm going to blow."

Seb took no heed of the friendly warning, as he was desperate to taste Andy's sweet seed and wanted to finish up quickly to get out of the frigid air. He furiously wanked while taking Andy's cock deeper into his throat with each bob of his head.

Andy tensed up and grabbed the back of Seb's head as he climaxed and shot wad after wad of thick, white cream into the counter-hand's warm and welcoming mouth.

Seb wasn't expecting such a big load and swallowed it down as best he could but, even so, he had it leaking from his mouth and down his chin. The salty-sweet taste in his mouth was all he needed to let his own load spurt out and onto the freezer floor between Andy's legs.

Andy pulled Seb up to his feet and kissed him deeply, enjoying the taste of his own cum in Seb's mouth.

"We'd better get out of here before we freeze our balls off," said Andy pulling up his pants.

"I can keep them warm for you," replied Seb with his ever-present cheeky grin.

"Enough time for that later. Now we better clean it up before it freezes solid."

"It's fine; we can just chip it off and serve it in the iced coffee. I'm sure the customers will love it!"

Andy just laughed, knowing full well that Seb was most probably right. After all, the seed cakes still continued to do quite a brisk business. So much so that all the boys in the café were contributing to the mix to ensure that their customers' demands were met. Admittedly, he'd been a little taken aback when Dom first told him about their side range for a select clientele but he had quickly seen their appeal after sampling a few.

They finished getting dressed and hopped outside to warm up a bit before finishing restocking the freezer. When they were done, they arranged to finish their playtime in a more temperate setting later that evening, where their appendages were more likely to fall off from overuse than frostbite.

* * *

After scouring the city for the perfect venue, Dom and Ben knew they had found it when they stepped onto the rooftop terrace of The Grand Babylon Hotel. It had actually been one of their café regulars, Danny, who'd suggested they have a look at the place after he'd overheard the boys discussing their troubles in finding the right location. He'd been to a few functions there and had been rather impressed by the food, the staff and the view.

They arranged to meet with the event coordinator the following week to discuss the possibility of hosting their wedding there in late June. They were warmly greeted in the lobby by Charlotte, an immaculately polished, blonde, middle-aged woman – her exact age being a closely guarded secret between her and her trusted 'beauty consultant' but to be fair the man did do fantastic work with barely a hint of plasticity about her face at all. She took them up to the terrace, where they were instantly blown away by the spectacular view out over the harbor, and while enjoying a scrumptious lunch of spinach and ricotta gnocchi with garlic mushrooms, they worked out the finer details. They were delighted to discover that the hiring fee included, not only the honeymoon suite for them to stay in over the wedding period, but two other deluxe rooms for their most special guests as well. The package also gave them access to the spa and a complimentary couple's massage to help alleviate those stressful pre-wedding jitters – sadly there was no guaranteed happy ending.

They decided almost immediately to give a room each to Seb and Adam, assuming that Adam would bring Steve, but who Seb would end up sharing his bed with was anyone's guess really.

Once they had set the date and location they were forced to finalize the guest list and invitations. It was hard working out whom to invite, and figuring out who wouldn't be mortally offended by not being asked.

After the list had been whittled down to a more manageable number they secured the services of a talented graphic artist to design the place cards and formal invitations. They wanted to add a more personal touch and were looking into the cost of calligraphist when they learned that Adam had beautiful penmanship – not so startling a revelation given the many occasions he had ably demonstrated how adept he was with his hands. So, he was soon tasked with the tiresome chore but was handsomely compensated for his troubles with a romantic candlelit dinner for him and Steve at their favorite restaurant.

They posted the invitations out the following week, allowing people up to three months to respond, and were overjoyed when they started receiving thrilled acceptances practically straight away. Indeed, some of their friends seemed to be even more excited than they were at the prospect of the marriage, which they found highly amusing and thoroughly touching. Ben and Dom were looking forward to standing up and expressing their love in front of their nearest and dearest and then running away to fuck like depraved bunnies after it was all done.

* * *

All throughout their wedding preparations, Dom and Ben continued their search for a new place to live, their landlord having chosen this most inopportune time to accept an offer from a developer, who planned to tear down the entire building and put in luxury condos. It hadn't taken them completely by surprise as their district had been undergoing gentrification for quite some time now. Unfortunately, the eviction date was looming and they needed to find new lodgings before they were forced into something truly horrifying – like moving back in with their parents. Not that they didn't love their families, it was just that parents everywhere seemed to have an inability to treat their grown children as anything other than testy teenagers when finding themselves living under the same roof once more.

Their current apartment was cozy and had seen them through many good times – lively dinners, happy sleepovers and that birthday party that had turned into a bit of all-out orgy. Originally, they had thought to simply rent another apartment but, after speaking with their realtor friend Thomas, the idea of buying an apartment in an up-and-coming area seemed to be a much more sensible move. They had stayed in touch with Thomas after he'd helped Dom with buying the café. He'd become a regular customer, stopping by at least once a week for a banana muffin or butterscotch seed cake if the mood struck him. Their friendship had grown over time, and not only because of his stunning Nordic frame and equally beautiful nine-inch cock – although these were definitely encouraging factors in the friendship. They had become quite close, so when they needed real estate assistance he was easily their first choice.

Their business had been going exceptionally well for a while now and their savings had been piling up nicely. So, they trusted his advice and were soon looking through the listings of available properties to buy. They wanted something in a similar style to where they had been living, but with a few minor changes. Dom was keen for a bigger kitchen to potter about in, as well as more space to entertain, while Ben was after a second bedroom for guests that could double as a study.

Thomas had shown them a few places but nothing really grabbed them. It was also difficult finding the time with all the other preparations going on. They would have much preferred to take more time with such an important decision but it wasn't a luxury they had.

About three months before the wedding, Thomas came to them with the perfect solution. An apartment in his complex had just come on the market and fit all of their needs. The owner was anxious for a quick sale, after his somewhat creative approach to paying his taxes had come to light and he needed the cash to pay his substantial fines in order to avoid a spot of inconvenient incarceration. They eagerly went to visit and while they were touring the fitness facilities in the basement they noticed that the building seemed to have rather a lot of like-minded gentlemen living there. In fact there was so much cruising going on they could easily have been at Sweat Station, the gloriously gay gym next door to their café.

Once they got into the apartment itself, Thomas had a few calls to make so he just let them wander about the place at their leisure. They were admiring the view of the city from the terrace when they noticed that they could see directly down into the balcony below them, where two stunning examples of manhood were sunning themselves *au naturel*. They were about to turn away to give their potential neighbors some privacy when they saw the man on the left reach across and start playing with the other's exposed cock.

The man on the right soon returned the favor, with both cocks quickly becoming fully erect. Before too long the mutual masturbation turned into mutual fellatio. The boys knew they should look away but the scene unfolding below them was just too hot to ignore. The one that initiated the action was the more muscular of the two. He had cropped brown hair, dark tanned skin and a small tribal tattoo on his neck, while his companion was much paler with black hair and a neatly trimmed beard. Both of them also had quite sizeable pieces of equipment between their legs. As they kept watching, the brunette broke away, swiftly straddled the other and sat right down on the other's cock and started riding it with glee.

The voyeurism had them rather hard, so Dom undid his fly and pulled out his own manhood. He yanked down the back of Ben's cargo shorts and as he rubbed his leaking cock against the tight entrance, he spat into

his hand and used it as lubrication before forcing his way inside, all the while riveted by the sizzling scene happening beneath them. Dom had only just started pumping lightly when Thomas startled them by coming onto the terrace, not that they stopped.

Thomas had a quick look over the railing and after seeing what had gotten them so worked up, sank to his knees and pulled Ben's shorts all the way down so he could join in on the fun. Ben didn't protest in the slightest when he felt Thomas's face bury itself in his crotch and simply enjoyed the sensation of being worked on by two hunks at once.

Dom's cock and Thomas' mouth worked in conjunction to pleasure Ben and soon had his body tensed up in a powerful ejaculation. Ben began shooting down the realtor's eager throat, just as Dom gave a few last thrusts into Ben's contracting ass and deposited his load deep inside his fiancé. Thomas had been furiously wanking, as he sucked the last few drops of cum out of Ben, when he suddenly blew all over himself, coating his tie and navy-blue business shirt in white, manly goodness. He excused himself, leaving the boys to make themselves presentable, while he went inside to wash off the sticky substance before it left tell-tale stains on his clothes.

When Thomas returned they told him that they wanted to take the apartment. It was then the trio heard the very loud, unmistakable sounds of orgasm and peered over the edge to see the brunette on the balcony below spurting his juice all over the chest of his companion. When he was spent he looked directly up at the boys and gave them a sly wink. In that moment they knew they had definitely found the right place and made a vow to get to know their new neighbors better, preferably as soon as possible.

After they'd signed the contract the following Tuesday, they thanked Thomas properly with a bottle of rosé champagne and another very enthusiastic threesome.

Thomas was pleased everything had worked out for the boys and that they were practically neighbors. Indeed, the randy realtor wished that all his dealings ended in such a pleasant manner.

* * *

Now that their housing issues had been sorted they allowed themselves to focus fully on the wedding preparations. It was decided the following weekend should be devoted to shopping for suits and rings. Leaving Andy and Max – their new counterhand – to deal with the late afternoon Saturday shift, Ben, Dom, Seb and Adam headed off to the main shopping district, which was home to quite a few jewelers and bespoke tailors – they didn't want to buy off the rack, after all. The foursome browsed in a few different stores before coming across a shop window with the most exquisite tailored suits on display. Popping inside the rather cosy shop, they encountered the owner in the middle of a fitting with a rather portly gentleman.

"Be with you in a moment," he said in the most charming British accent. All the boys swooned just a little. It didn't hurt that the tailor was quite handsome, tall and lean with alabaster skin, dark brown floppy hair, and gentle, bright-blue eyes. Dressed in an impeccably cut, light-gray, three-piece suit, he was the very vision of gentility and refinement.

The boys were impressed with the diplomatic way the tailor was handling the demands of his current client, trying to steer him towards a more flattering style and color for his heavier frame.

Once he had allayed all his customer's concerns, and sent him on his merry way, the man turned his attentions to the foursome. He introduced himself as Daniel Applewhite and immediately made reference to his obviously foreign tongue. He explained that he had immigrated a few years ago after receiving his training on Savile Row. Despite his relatively young age of thirty he was rather accomplished and had quite the reputation. It would also be fair to say that he spent a great deal of time around men's inseams – with and without his trusty tape measure.

Dom and Ben explained what they were after for themselves and their best men. They tried on various jackets and pants to get an idea of cut and color and once they had decided, Daniel finished off by taking precise measurements of all of them. He measured Dom and Ben first as they were eager to be off to a certain jeweler's in the next block, where there was a pair of platinum rings they'd rather liked.

None of the boys seemed to mind the tailor's nimble fingers lightly grazing against their crotches as he went about his work – he was only being thorough in his job, after all. After Daniel had finished with him Adam popped next door to grab some coffees, leaving Seb alone with the young tailor. Seb noticed that Daniel's hands seemed to be lingering longer about his crotch than was strictly necessary or professional. As usual he never needed much encouragement and the front of his pants soon started to bulge in a most unsubtle manner.

"I'm terribly sorry but I seem to be having trouble with this last measurement," said Daniel politely. "Perhaps there is something I can do to help alleviate the problem?"

Without waiting for an answer he deftly undid Seb's button fly and had the tanned, and increasingly erect, nine-inch cock in his mouth in a surprisingly quick space of time. He practically inhaled it.

As is often the case, one can never judge a book by its cover and this well-put-together young man turned out to have as big an appetite for cock as Seb did, which a great many men had had the pleasure to experience.

So engrossed was Daniel in his task, of draining Seb's manhood back down to a more manageable size, he didn't hear Adam returning with the drinks.

Not one to miss an opportunity, Adam set down the coffees and swiftly had his pants down, presenting himself to the hungry tailor.

Daniel looked up and grabbed hold of Adam's beautifully growing cock while still masterfully attending to the one in his throat. He pulled Adam closer in and then alternated between the two delicious dicks, lavishing them both with his talented tongue.

The front of Daniel's trousers had also tented up by this time, darkening a little where the precum had started to soak through, giving Seb cause to get down on the floor and release the tailor's cock into the air. Seb sighed with appreciation when the extremely thick seven inches of uncut manhood popped out into the open and speedily went to work lapping up all the tasty juice dripping from the cockhead and all over his chunky, English foreskin.

Daniel moaned in appreciation as Seb worked his magic on his member. The encounter was being made all that much hotter by the very real prospect of a random customer suddenly barging in on them at any moment.

Seb abruptly stood up, pulling Daniel to his feet at the same time. He started kissing him, bringing Adam into them as well; their three cocks rubbing up against each other as their tongues explored each other's mouths. Seb and Adam unbuttoned Daniel's vest and shirt to reveal the tailor's defined torso and almost translucently pale, soft white skin – well he was English after all.

Adam removed his t-shirt and pressed his skin up against Daniel's as they resumed kissing. Seb took this opportunity to whip the tailor's pants down, returning to his knees he spread Daniel's cheeks wide and rimmed him hard.

Daniel eagerly pushed back to take full advantage of Seb's skilled mouth and relaxed his sphincter further to allow Seb to penetrate even deeper into his passage.

Adam joined Seb on the floor and gave Daniel the same special treatment the tailor had given him earlier.

Daniel placed one hand on the back of the head in front of him and one of the head behind, savagely pulling them in towards him and encouraging them in their willing work.

After Seb had thoroughly worshipped Daniel's ass, he got to his feet, grabbed protection and lubrication from his satchel, suited up and slowly sunk his cock between the Brit's firm, white ass cheeks. Seb had thought to start slowly but Daniel had other ideas and was soon slamming his hips backwards into Seb's crotch, clearly desperate to be ploughed hard. Seb loved Daniel's zeal and ably fucked the tailor as hard as he could. The thrusting became too violent for Adam to continue sucking so he stood up and supported Daniel's body. The tailor's cries of pleasure rang out through the small shop as Seb ruthlessly pumped away.

Daniel's moans got even louder and Adam looked down to see that he was starting to blow without even touching himself – something that Adam had frequently heard about but never seen in the flesh. Quick as a flash, Adam squatted down and took the erupting cock in his mouth allowing Daniel to pump the rest of his substantial load down Adam's slick throat. When he had drained Daniel dry, Adam stood back up and gave him a deep, hungry kiss.

Seb then hastily pulled out, unwrapped his throbbing member and proceeded to blow all over Daniel's exposed ass. The thick, white cum leaked down over the Englishman's cheeks – now a rosy-pink color from all that fierce pounding.

Daniel took a firm grasp of Adam's solid manhood and briskly wanked him until he blew all over the carpeted floor and onto Daniel's polished shoes.

The tailor swiftly grabbed a nearby spare cloth to tidy himself and the others up and clean away the sticky seed that was splashed about on the floor. The way he did it, without any muss or fuss, suggested that this may not have been the first, and was unlikely to be the last, such encounter Daniel had had at work.

Once they were all reclothed it was back to business, as Daniel resumed his professional manner and organized a date for the final fitting. Daniel suggested to the boys that they may wish to drop by another day, closer to closing time so that he could give them a more private fitting, which, of course, they eagerly agreed to.

True to their word, Seb and Adam returned the following Monday just before six in the evening. Daniel was just ushering the last of his customers out and discreetly locked the front door after the boys had entered.

"This time gentlemen, I'd like both of your gorgeous cocks inside me if you don't mind."

Needless to say, they didn't and Daniel contentedly rode them until he was red raw…

* * *

Among the many things that still needed to be decided and confirmed before the wedding was the photographer. Dom and Ben had an abundance of suggestions from friends but they were still unsure of exactly who to go with. Seb suggested they go see his cousin Spencer, an up and coming photographer who had recently done quite a few high profile fashion shoots. Anyone who'd met the cousins could see the family resemblance straight away. Both lads sported bronzed skin, blue eyes and the same cheeky grin. They also shared the same size of juicy, uncut cock, which they had discovered after doing more than a few comparisons whilst growing up – let's just say they had been more than kissing cousins. At just a couple of years older than Seb, but just as cock hungry as his cousin, Spencer was slightly more muscular, with brown hair and a sprinkling of light chest hair.

Dom and Ben made an appointment to see Spencer at his studio to discuss their needs. His loft apartment was rather light and airy with lots of open space, easily transforming into wildly different kinds of sets for his various shoots. The boys noticed the huge king-sized bed with all manner of props around it, ranging from those likely to be found in a hardcore fetish film though to more innocent apparel. Spencer explained that he also did high-class boudoir photos for some of his more discerning clients.

Spencer fixed them something to drink as they sat down to discuss their ideas for the wedding. The red wine flowed freely as they talked about the venue and certain shots they were after. The conversation turned back towards Spencer's more intimate work and somehow they ended up agreeing to do one or two playful shots just to see if they liked his style. Ben and Dom hopped on the bed and started to cuddle and kiss with Spencer giving them slight directions. The wine had lowered their inhibitions, not that they usually had that many, and most of their clothing was quickly cast aside. They continued making out with relish, barely aware of the flash of the camera and appreciative noises made by Spencer as he most definitely approved of what was happening on his bed.

Down to just their underwear, the boys were rolling around on the bed, precum seeping through the material as their excited cocks rubbed against each other. Ben moved down dragging off Dom's blue and white briefs. He hungrily devoured Dom's thick eight inches, eagerly licking up the stickiness on his cockhead and working the shaft with his mouth and throat.

By this point Spencer had put the camera down, left it running on auto capture while releasing his own hard cock from its restrictive covering of jeans, wanking happily as he watched the two muscular men enjoying each other's bodies.

Dom spun around into a sixty-nine, so he could help himself to his fiancé's mouth-watering meat. A move both of them appreciated given the resulting moans.

Spencer didn't want to interrupt them and was more than content to enjoy the show as the cocksucking naturally progressed into mutual rimming.

After about fifteen minutes or so Ben couldn't take any more of the probing of Dom's tongue and begged him to fuck him. Dom flipped Ben over onto his back on the bed, spread the fleshy, white cheeks, placed his cockhead at the moist entrance and eased himself inside. He worked the ass open, sinking further and further into the passage. Once he was balls-deep he started with a gentle rhythm, slowly sliding in and out of Ben making him writhe and moan with each tender thrust.

Just as he was about to speed up his pace he felt hands parting his own muscular buttocks, followed closely by the sensation of warm breath on his hole. He looked around and saw Spencer had tired of being a spectator and had buried his face between his ass cheeks. Never one to turn down a good rimming he tilted his hips forward to allow Spencer further access before sliding back further into Ben. He savored the feeling of Spencer's tongue searching in his ass, probing deep, trying to taste all of him, while his own bare cock was exploring the smooth insides of his fiancé.

Dom enjoyed the feeling of warmth at both ends for quite some time but his ass demanded something more substantial.

"Why don't you make better use of that fine cock of yours?" he asked Spencer.

The photographer was up in a jiffy and rapidly retrieved lube and a condom from the drawers by the bed and was suited up and ready to go in practically no time at all. Dom leaned forward to give Ben a long lingering kiss, which opened up his ass in preparation for the sizeable cock about to invade it. Spencer generously applied the lube before slipping his latex covered manhood into the tight ring. His previous experience had taught him to be well prepared as his was not a cock to be taken lightly. There was an initial resistance as Dom adjusted to the thick member pushing its way inside but once he'd relaxed Spencer slid all the way in, consequently pushing Dom deeper into Ben which they all appreciated.

Spencer then set the pace, violently slamming into Dom's beautiful ass, causing Dom to plough into Ben's

ass with equal force. The loft echoed with the sounds of their enthusiastic play…the encouraging dirty talk, hips hitting buttocks and guttural grunts of pleasure.

Ben was in heaven with the weight of the two men bearing down on him, as his ass was stretched in a most pleasurable way. Unfortunately, all good things must come to an end.

Dom soon found himself at the edge of orgasm, thanks in no small part to Spencer's constant pounding of his prostate. He bent down to kiss Ben as he gave a few last quick thrusts into Ben's beautiful butt and began filling it with his salty-sweet seed.

Ben loved the reassuringly familiar sensation of Dom's throbbing cock as his balls emptied their hot load. Ben increased the speed of his jacking off so that he could have his own sweet release. The feeling of Dom's still erect cock firmly inside him was all he needed his blow all over his lean, defined stomach and solid chest.

Dom then leaned down onto Ben and gently kissed him, as Spencer slowly pulled out. Spencer ripped off his condom and started wanking while watching the boys once more. After a few minutes Dom remembered they had an audience and turned over onto his back as well, pulling Spencer down on top of them and into a three-way kiss. Ben reached down and grabbed a hold of Spencer's cock while Dom grasped his balls and pulled down firmly, as they worked together to help the photographer have his own happy ending. The cocky couple kept kissing him as they expertly played with his crotch. Several extremely enjoyable minutes later, Spencer was unloading all over their sweaty bodies, before collapsing down onto the two of them. They lay there for a while enjoying the warmth and stickiness as their cum mixed together between their slick bodies.

After half an hour or so, the buzzer to Spencer's apartment sounded and roused the trio into action. He hustled the boys into the shower while he attended to the door. Thankfully, it was just a delivery of size 14 stilettos, a crate of stuffed animals and a glitter cannon for an upcoming project – drag queen shoots were the best. Once they were dressed, he kissed the boys goodbye and told them he'd send them some prints of their shoot and then they could decide if they wanted to book him.

Later, after viewing the images of their fervent lovemaking, they had no doubts this was the man to capture the magic of their special day. Plus the photos would make the perfect thank you cards for some of their more intimate acquaintances.

* * *

Among their many duties, Seb and Adam were tasked with organizing the joint bachelor party. Even though their first thoughts tended towards a good old-fashioned orgy, they thought they should put in just a little more effort. They debated about what form the party should take but they both agreed that the evening should ultimately end up at Stallions – the number one male strip club in the city. To make sure that everyone would have an awesome evening they took it upon themselves to personally choose the dancers that would be entertaining them on the evening in question – a dirty job but somebody had to do it.

They went along early on a Friday night to talk to the manager Roberta, about hiring a private room and to find out who amongst her stable of men would be the most suited to their needs. Roberta insisted that all of her staff would be more than able to satisfy any particular requests they had, but she thought it best if the boys caught that night's show and made the decision for themselves. So, in the interests of being thorough they loaded up with cocktails and a bunch of singles and settled in to hold their informal auditions. As the night wore on it was increasingly obvious that Roberta's hiring practices included a minimum requirement when it came to their ability to fill their underwear. In fact, all the men on display appeared to be a size-queen's wet dream. Now, while Stallions had quite the selection of erotic entertainers, there were only three that really caught their eyes – Cody, Sam and Brock.

They were three very different looks but all exuded their own charm. Cody was only nineteen but had certainly been around the block a few times – not to mention the various back alleys and gutters along the way. He loved to dance and was a whore for attention, so was rather suited to the profession. Cody was quite cute with his lean, twinkish build, short light-brown hair and hazel eyes but was not, at first glance, ideal stripper material. When he undressed down to his bright red jockstrap, however, it was clear that the gods had undeniably blessed the boy. Indeed, the fabric of his underwear strained almost to breaking point, struggling to contain the eleven-inch uncut monster contained within. The almost indecent bulge easily enthralled the spectators, eager for a glimpse of his amazing appendage. It was a wonder his sense of balance wasn't thrown off by having to lug the thing around.

At thirty-three years old, Sam was one of the oldest performers at Stallions, but still captivated the crowd with his middle-eastern looks, wavy, black hair and dark sultry eyes. His not inconsiderable package contained a nine and a half inch uncut treasure, which only served to add to his appeal. Adam thought he recognized Sam from somewhere but couldn't place him right away.

Regardless, he easily made their short list of entertainers for the party.

Brock was of Eurasian heritage and certainly knew how to move. He had cropped, bleach-blond hair, mesmerizing bright-green eyes and silky-smooth, lightly tanned skin. Brock looked a little younger than his twenty-four years and had been stripping for about five years. Like his fellow dancers, he was extremely well endowed and the club's patrons often admired his ten inches of uncut glory.

Seb and Adam happily paid for private dances with the trio to conduct a more intimate inspection. Once in the room, the boys sat down in separate armchairs as the strippers put on quite the show, dancing with each other, with their erections rather noticeable through their skimpy outfits. Despite the apparent 'no touching' policy the strippers seemed more than keen to give Seb and Adam a more hands-on experience. In moments they had gone from simply watching to keenly participating, as Cody planted himself on Seb's lap with Sam doing the same to Adam.

Brock continued to dance around them, leaning in to kiss Adam then Seb in turn, as his co-workers did their best to give the boys their money's worth.

It was at this point that Adam realized he knew Sam from one his recent favorite online videos, where Sam played a strict coach disciplining his thoroughly naughty college football team. He tried not to let his inner fanboy show but after a few minutes of Sam grinding away in his lap he couldn't help but blurt out "I loved you in Freshmen Fever!"

"Always a pleasure to meet a fan." Sam said appreciatively, before sliding off Adam, sinking to his knees to release Adam's cock from his jeans and swallowing him to the base in one seamless, expertly executed move.

Seb was too distracted to notice what was happening to Adam as he had his hands full, so to speak, with the impressive meat of both Brock and Cody being waved in his face. So, he did what any good boy would do and did his very best to please both men at once. This proved quite the challenge even for a lad of his particular talents. He tried to eat as much of them as he could, alternating between the two tasty cocks, all the while thinking about how it would feel to have both of these monsters fighting inside his tight, tanned ass at the same time, stretching him every which way.

By now Adam had switched places with Sam and was returning the favor by quite happily feasting away on the delicious, dark meat before him. Sam ran his hands through Adam's shoulder-length red hair, roughly pushing his head deeper into his crotch.

Sadly, they knew their time was limited and had to wrap things up before the next show, as much as they'd all have liked to have continued on, Adam and Seb being much more attractive than their usual customers. Brock went to his knees and started giving Seb a much-appreciated blowjob while Cody continued to force himself down Seb's throat. It didn't take much before Seb was gushing into Brock's experienced mouth.

Sam had also resumed his sucking of Adam's fine cock and soon had the pleasure of tasting his milky load, as it spurted into his mouth and slid down the back of his throat.

The boys were disappointed that they couldn't help the strippers out in same way but they understood the importance of their needing to wait to the end of the evening, so as to not diminish the boys' ability to perform throughout the night.

Afterwards, they briefly chatted about the upcoming soirée and what they wanted. The boys had no issues at all, especially after they saw a photo of the happy couple, and even suggested a few things that they'd like to add in for free. All too soon the strippers had to be on their way, so they quickly settled on a price and the date in about a month's time.

* * *

Ben and Dom had narrowed the list of cakes for the wedding down to three choices – raspberry coconut sponge, honey fruitcake and a caramel mud cake. Andy had already become quite a trusted member of their crew and with his culinary skills he was a natural choice to aid Dom with the wedding cake. About six weeks before the wedding, Ben was off at a weekend workshop in the country, run by his yoga center, so Dom took advantage of the free time to try out the chosen recipes.

Andy and Dom were cooking up a storm in the new apartment. It had been a scorching hot day and despite the air-conditioning, the kitchen was like a sauna. Andy had stripped down to his loose navy-blue boxers, while Dom was only in his apron – as usual – not that Andy appeared to mind in the slightest.

They had prepared the batter for all three cakes, taking little tastes of each mixture as they went, and were just getting ready to pour them into the tins for baking. Andy's big, chocolate-brown nipples were poking out in a tantalizing fashion around the edge of his apron and Dom couldn't resist putting a dollop of caramel onto the left one with the silver tablespoon, before bending forward and licking it off. Andy looked shocked for all of one second before he grabbed another spoon and put a splodge of the raspberry sauce on his other nipple and waited for Dom to clean it off too. Dom willingly complied but then kept licking and sucking long after the raspberry had been cleaned away. When he'd finished, Andy picked up the closest jar, lifted up Dom's apron and covered the thick Greek cock with golden-brown honey. Andy bent down and did his very best to remove every last trace of the sticky substance. Dom appreciated Andy's dedication, as his cock worked in and out of the very soft, warm mouth, the gifted tongue flicking fervently over the sticky meat.

Without warning, Dom yanked Andy up to a standing position and pushed him roughly up against the counter sealing his lips in a lustful kiss. Andy's cock was poking out through the opening of his boxers and rubbing up against Dom as they kissed. Dom reached down and slowly wanked their two cocks together, the precum from both mixing together as his hand moved up and down at a steady pace. Andy's smooth black skin slid back and forth against Dom's as the heat in the kitchen caused sweat to drip from their athletic bodies.

Dom then lifted Andy up onto the bench and whisked his boxers off, pushing him backwards so that he was naked with his legs in the air. Dom had moved the ingredients aside but there was still as gummy mess spreading beneath Andy's back as Dom went to work. Andy squirmed with pleasure as Dom alternated between sucking the big, black cock and eating out the beautiful bubble butt.

Andy had his hands firmly on Dom's shoulders and neck, digging his fingers into the skin as Dom savagely attacked his sensitive groin area with an onslaught of licks and bites. When Dom started scraping his stubble across the heavy ball sack Andy's eyes rolled back into his head in ecstasy.

Dom moved back down to Andy's ass and used his tongue and fingers to open up his employee's tight ring. Happy with his progress, Dom swiftly went to the fridge to grab a few items.

"Don't you think about moving." Dom warned Andy.

"Wouldn't dream of it," replied Andy, who was more than content with his current predicament.

Dom returned to the counter with a bunch of washed vegetables and a bottle of extra virgin olive oil. He poured some of the oil directly into Andy's exposed hole, using his fingers to work it further inside. With his other hand Dom grabbed a carrot and proceeded to slowly violate Andy with it, gradually picking up speed as Andy's moans reverberated throughout the apartment. From carrots Dom moved on to cucumbers, zucchinis and other similarly shaped produce, each increasing in size.

Andy had never done anything like this before and was getting off on the novelty of it almost as much as the sensation of the thick vegetables stretching and teasing his ass.

After he was finished with each one Dom put them aside in a pile, with the aim of cooking up a very special savory cake when they were done. Dom finally came to the end of his supply of surrogate dildos – a disturbingly long and thick sweet potato. He pushed it in as deep as he dared into Andy's well-worked ass, poking and probing as Andy grunted and groaned. Dom took Andy's cock in hand and jacked him off to the same rhythm as the vegetable sliding in and out. He could sense that Andy was close so he revved up the pace and started brutally slamming it in, to give him the relief he so richly deserved. Andy's body started to shudder and shake as he ejaculated, his semen flying out of his cock and splattering all over the kitchen – the sink, the window…even the microwave didn't escape the blitz.

Dom gently removed the vegetable from Andy's abused hole, grateful that the fierce contractions hadn't crushed it to pieces. He then took himself in hand and raced towards his own burst of pleasure. It took about all of thirty seconds before he was spraying his load over Andy's wet and sticky body. Dom bent over the bench, leaning onto Andy as he lightly kissed him. Once they'd recovered from their exertions Dom helped Andy off of the bench, supporting him as the blood rushed back into his solid legs. He then led him off to the shower so they could well and truly clean up before attempting to deal with the mess they'd just made of the kitchen.

It took them longer than expected to get back to work, as their shower-time transformed into bedroom-time and then back to the bathroom to clean up again, with a great deal of frantic fucking in between. By the time they eventually made it back to the kitchen the mess of ingredients had begun to solidify and it took more than a bit of elbow grease to get everything back into tip-top condition. Not that either of them regretted the cause of the chaos for a second.

Before they started cleaning Dom quickly put together the savory cake he'd been thinking about earlier so that it baked while they worked. When they were done they sat down to eat it, with a fresh green salad, and were both surprised by the zesty and altogether scrumptious flavor.

* * *

As the wedding date approached, Dom and Ben found their stress levels rising as they dealt with all the fiddly little details that tend to drive people in such situations thoroughly mad. This in turn caused little fights between them where they snapped at each other over the most trivial of things. The only good part was that the resulting make-up sex was always worth it. Sometimes they couldn't even wait for the end and started to fuck mid-fight, which always ended the argument in a most pleasing fashion.

The seating plan was a complete nightmare, as they struggled to remember who hated who and the age-old dilemma of who to put at the table the furthest away – people could so be sensitive to perceived slights. Then there was the drama of trying to cater to all the allergies and food lifestyle choices – astonishing given some of the things they knew that their friends put in their mouths recreationally. Honestly, it was a wonder that people could even eat any more. Dom was glad that he was only preparing the wedding cake, as he would have gone quietly insane trying to please everyone. Fortunately, the hotel had been able to accommodate the demands of their more finicky guests. The boys had been vaguely tempted to put some of their more fussy friends at the back in the corner with a bowl of water and a packet of peanuts and encouraged them to fight it out Hunger Games style….such daydreams helped them through the tougher times.

Next on their – thankfully dwindling – list was finding a celebrant to help them create the most perfect day.

As it happened, Ben had encountered a pleasantly plump woman named Margaret at his recent yoga retreat – while yoga wasn't Dom's cup of tea he certainly appreciated all the new and interesting positions that Ben was now able to get himself into. Ben's newfound flexibility was due in no small part to the good-looking yoga instructor Derek, who'd been very keen to help Ben align all of his chakras, no matter how many times he had to pound Ben's tight bubble butt to do it. Unsurprisingly, it hadn't been the first time that Derek had seduced a student but Ben had been more than willing to submit to his teacher's advances. In fact, he had actively encouraged him with an array of scandalously skimpy gym shorts that he wore, however briefly, for every session they had.

Margaret was spiritual, without being annoying about it, and had assisted at many such unions, so was able to read the couple well enough to cater to their needs. She was also able to help them wade through the confusing amount of advice they'd received from their friends and family. Indeed, everyone seemed to have an opinion on what they should do. It was almost as if they were trying to live vicariously through them…most strange.

They decided to write their own vows and have a few readings from friends but nothing overly religious, as it wasn't particularly to their tastes. As for music, they wanted something simple, yet elegant, to be played as they walked each other down the aisle.

For the reception, however, they had decided upon a DJ friend of theirs with whom they'd grown up – Jonathan. A very talented and handsome man, he'd started off just playing friend's parties but had rapidly risen through the clubbing ranks. Jonathon knew how to read a crowd, playing many different types of venues from clubs to saunas and everything in between. They had danced to many of his sets in some of the hottest spots in the city – not to mention made out and fucked to his music in the privacy of their own home.

Jonathan was honored that the boys wanted to use him and asked them for a list of their favorite songs so he could prepare a set worthy of their event. In lieu of payment, he asked only to be kept swimming in champagne all night long and to be surrounded by beautiful boys – an artist needs his muses, after all. He knew by their circle of friends that the eye-candy level would be high and this wasn't likely to be a problem at all.

* * *

Seb and Adam had organized to have the bachelor party two weeks before the big day to eliminate the possibility of any of the participants being too hung-over or otherwise wrecked for the wedding. The evening started off in a fairly civilized manner with dinner at an upscale Italian restaurant, followed by cocktails at a bar just across the street. They had invited assorted friends of the couple and Dom's three brothers – Paul, Philippe and Dimitri. Later, the crowd thinned somewhat when it was time to move onto more adult pursuits – namely watching buff men remove their clothes for money in time to pop music. Dom's two older brothers had wives and children to get back to, but Dimitri, Dom's little brother, had no such attachments. He was the baby of the family and had always been indulged, with even Dom's strict father turning a blind eye to his youngest son's more rascally pursuits.

He was roughly the same build as Dom and shared the same Mediterranean complexion and striking green eyes but was quite content to let his hairiness run a tad more free than Dom. Dimitri worked on the docks just like his dad and other brothers. Unlike them, however, he was slightly more open sexually and was of the opinion that one warm, hospitable hole was as good as another. Having broken up with a long time girlfriend a few months back he was certainly in the mood to be sewing his wild oats in any field that would have them. Fortunately, his dark curly hair and emerald eyes ensured that he never wanted for company.

The others to continue on were the happy couple, Steve, Eric, Thomas and the rest of the boys from the café – except for Max who'd had a previous family engagement that he couldn't wriggle out of. They arrived at Stallions in quite high spirits, starting off in the main room with complimentary cocktails and enjoying the bevy of beautiful boys who were working the crowd, while their private room was being set up.

Brock, one of the dancers that Seb and Adam had handpicked, took an immediate shine to Dimitri. He came over and introduced himself before proceeding to give him a lap dance. Dimitri wasn't keen on getting too worked up in front of his brother and asked Brock if they could perhaps continue in a more concealed setting. Brock quickly hopped up, grabbed Dimitri by the hand and led him off to a private booth. Once there Brock wasted no time getting to work, swiftly stripping down to a tiny, blue jockstrap, pushing Dimitri down onto the black leather couch and jumping straight back onto his waiting lap.

Without the inhibition of having his brother there Dimitri gave into his natural masculine desires and began kissing Brock passionately as the stripper continued to grind into his crotch. Dimitri's wandering hands made their way to Brock's exposed ass and his fingers ventured towards the smooth, inviting hole.

Brock grabbed a hold of the young Greek's t-shirt and pulled it off to expose a beautifully hairy, solid chest. Brock sat back so that he could lick and bite Dimitri's erect, light-brown nipples, making him cry out in pleasure. He worked his way down towards the crotch and saw that the pants were noticeably curving outward with Dimitri's hard cock trying to escape.

Brock dexterously undid the jeans and promptly swallowed down the eight inches of juicy uncut manhood he found there. Brock didn't mind at all when Dimitri grabbed the back of his head and started to fuck his face with joy, he quite loved being treated in such a fashion but he had other plans in store for this particular customer.

After a while, Brock broke away and stood up and ignoring Dimitri's questioning look he grabbed some protection from the container by the door. Before Dimitri quite realized what was happening, Brock had slipped a condom on him, straddled him and taken his thick meat all the way to the base – the two footballers he'd had earlier that evening certainly easing the way. That being said, he was by no means loose as years of practice had given him excellent muscle control and he was easily able to milk a man dry with his wonderfully skilled ass.

Dimitri quickly recovered from the surprise and started thrusting his hips up to match the rhythm of Brock's movements. Brock tweaked Dimitri's nipples, which had become even more sensitive after the earlier biting, as he rode the cock like a champion. By this time Brock's own cock was straining to break out of the surprisingly strong pouch of the jockstrap. Dimitri moved his right hand from Brock's hip and proceeded to stroke the dick through the moist material. The bulge continued to grow even further and Dimitri began to wonder exactly how big a giant was hiding inside. His curiosity was soon satisfied when he freed it and had ten glorious inches of uncut cock in his hand.

"Fucking hell!" he exclaimed.

"I'll take that as a compliment." Brock smirked as he kept bouncing up and down.

"How do you not pass out from blood loss?"

"Let me show you." Brock said with a wicked grin as he hopped off Dimitri and sunk to his knees. He pulled off Dimitri's jeans, lifted up his firm, muscular legs up and shoved his tongue into the hot, hairy hole.

Dimitri loved being roughly rimmed and Brock was doing a superb job. He even moved his ass down over the edge of the lounge so that Brock could force his way in even deeper.

Unseen by Dimitri, Brock had grabbed another condom and was suiting himself up while he probed the velvety passage with his tongue. When he was ready he stood up and slowly guided his many inches deep inside.

Dimitri involuntarily contracted around the invader. It had been a while since he'd had anything, let alone something that big, inside him . Brock leant forward and kissed him fervently, their matching green eyes locked in an intense stare, which helped Dimitri to relax and let his ass be penetrated fully.

Brock started thrusting slowly to allow Dimitri's very full ass to adjust to the magnificent meat inside him. The stripper knew all too well that his cock could cause an unfortunate injury if not handled with care, although once he got an ass warmed up all bets were off.

Not long after, Dimitri grabbed at Brock's hips, encouraging him to pound harder and faster. He wanted to be ridden rough and used like the dirty boy he truly was.

Brock picked up Dimitri's legs and supported him in the air with only his head and shoulders resting on the couch as he slammed mercilessly into the Greek boy's tight ass. Dimitri's cock whacked against his hairy stomach with every thrust, leaking delicious precum all over his black snail trail making it stick to his dark skin. He was moaning quite loudly with the pummeling his ass was getting but fortunately Roberta had long ago taken the sensible precaution of having all the private booths and function rooms soundproofed to enable the patrons to enjoy themselves fully without having to worry about their fun being overheard.

In quite an unexpected show of strength, Brock suddenly bent forward and picked up Dimitri fully and continued fucking him in the air, only supporting him from below with his muscular arms. The new position caused Brock's massive cock to penetrate even further inside, making Dimitri swear profusely in pleasure. They continued on until Brock's arms began to tire at which point he spun around and sat on the couch, kissing Dimitri as he continued to grind deep inside him.

Brock was secretly impressed at Dimitri's ability to take him for such a long time without begging for a break – no doubt a happy by-product of the many cocktails he'd consumed earlier. They continued on like this for quite a while, kissing passionately while writhing together. It was then that their fucking became much more sensual than rough.

After a while, even all the alcohol in the world wouldn't have allowed too much more punishment of his ass. Brock recognizing the need in Dimitri's eyes grabbed a hold of the beautiful uncut cock bouncing between them and started to wank him as he increased the pace of his invasion. It didn't take long before the endless deep probing stimulated Dimitri's prostate beyond the point of no return and he started to spurt his thick, white seed all over himself and Brock. The sight of all that delicious cream splashing all over them, coupled with the contracting of Dimitri's ravished ass, was all the inspiration Brock needed and he began to fill the condom with his own load. Dimitri collapsed forward onto Brock, just resting there as he felt the throbbing of Brock's cock becoming less and less strong. Once they had finished panting they resumed kissing, with Brock slowly sliding out of Dimitri's grateful passage.

"Look, I'm finishing up soon. Did you wanna go for a drink?"

"Sure, but I should say goodbye to my brother and his friends first."

"I wouldn't worry about that, I'm pretty sure they have their hands full." said Brock with a mischievous knowing look. "By the way my name's actually Jay."

"Nice to meet you," replied Dimitri before going in for another long deep and passionate kiss.

* * *

Meanwhile, back in the private function room, the rest of the boys were enjoying themselves immensely. Not only were they being entertained by the dancing prowess of Cody and Sam, but Roberta had put on quite the spread, with a great many sweet and savory treats on offer. Dom was genuinely surprised at the quality of the food given their somewhat seedy environs. Of particular note were the Kaluha Cookie Shots, which were being consumed at a rather rapid rate.

Ben and Dom were impressed with how the whole evening had been organized. What they didn't know was that Seb had actually arranged for Brock to distract Dimitri so that the group could have a more highly charged evening without worrying about awkward situations with family members. Although he hadn't planned on just how well the two would get along.

As the evening wore on, the group became more inebriated and lively. So much so, that Thomas and Seb engaged in a spot of impromptu wrestling, which led to them bumping into Eric and Adam and in turn to them accidentally spilling a bottle of red wine all over the celebrating bachelors.

They apologized profusely, of course, and hastened to strip off Ben and Dom's clothes in order to soak them before they stained. Seb went off to fetch Roberta, who proved adept at dealing with soiled garments – not all that unexpected given what usually went on at the club.

This left Ben and Dom standing there in their underwear as their friends looked on in amusement. When Seb returned he announced that it was time for their bachelor party surprise. The boys were led up onto the stage where Cody and Sam had been dancing and placed onto two wooden seats that they hadn't paid attention to earlier. Seb motioned for the strippers to come up and give the boys their celebratory lap dances. Dom and Ben were far too distracted by the gyrating men and alcohol to notice that their seats had an assortment of strategically located leather restraints.

Cody was doing his best to keep Dom occupied, as was Sam with Ben, so that the others could discreetly fasten them to their chairs. Even if they had noticed, it was extremely doubtful that they would have cared, their underwear showing quite clearly their enjoyment of their respective lap dances. Once they were firmly secured, Seb gave Cody and Sam the long-awaited signal. At which point they promptly jumped up and roughly ripped the underwear off of the unsuspecting, restrained duo. They were confused at first, then slightly outraged seeing that their jocks were a fairly pricey brand. Their anger changed to a nervous excitement when they both realized that all the other members of their party now appeared to be naked and surrounding them in a cozy circle.

"Time for your real surprise!" exclaimed Seb with his customary cheeky grin.

The boys weren't quite sure what to expect but when Dom caught sight of a pile of condoms and several bottles of lube that had miraculously appeared on the buffet table he had a fair idea of what was coming their way.

Their friends stood by watching and stroking themselves as Cody and Sam rolled the condoms on each other in a rather seductive display.

"Who's first?" demanded Cody, brandishing his cock like a dangerous weapon…not to say it couldn't do a great deal of damage if he felt so inclined. After seeing Ben's extremely worried look, Dom bravely volunteered to take one for the team as it were. This meant that Sam set his sights on Ben's inviting round bubble butt. Ben was tremendously relieved that his ass would have the chance to be warmed up by Sam's decent-sized dick before being subjected to Cody's monster.

The boys were only attached to the chairs by straps around their arms and chests, so when Cody and Sam moved forward they were easily able to lift up the legs of their prisoners to reveal their vulnerable holes. Not wanting to be mean to their willing captives, they were exceptionally liberal when applying the lube and eased their way ever so gradually into the boys' taut asses. The alcohol and hotness of the situation helped a great deal and the strippers soon felt Dom and Ben start to relax as their thrusting became more forceful. Cody unrelentingly penetrated into Dom further than any man had before, rendering the groom-to-be almost delirious with pleasure.

The others were playing in little groups of threes and fours, kissing, fingering and wanking each other, as they continued to watch Cody fucking Dom and Ben being violated by Sam. The strippers were certainly enthusiastic in their work. Not content to simply pump away, they were tweaking the boys' nipples, kissing them, raking their fingernails across the bare flesh and stimulating their bodies in every way.

After what seemed like hours to the tied twosome, Cody and Sam stopped and switched partners. For Dom this was a bit of relief as Sam's cock was much easier to deal with than Cody's had been. As amazing as it had felt there was only so much a man could withstand before fear of permanent injury set in. Ben's adventure, however, was just beginning as Cody slid into him perhaps a tad more quickly than he'd intended causing the poor boy to cry out and momentarily see stars. Once the discomfort had abated, Ben began to rather enjoy the feeling of being so completely full of cock and encouraged Cody to fuck him even harder. The well-hung young man was more than happy to comply and started fucking like he wanted to tear Ben in two. Ben half-regretted the request in between the bursts of ecstasy as the monster meat opened him up as never before.

Cody and Sam happily continued to plough the boys for a good long while, until they decided it was time to let the group have their fun. They graciously moved aside for the men, who were more than keen to have their turn at defiling the happy couple. One by one, their friends took their place, suited up and had their wicked way with them.

The strippers helped out by bringing drinks over to Ben and Dom, so that they could keep up their alcohol levels and hopefully numb any soreness caused by the overuse of their asses.

To tell the truth, the boys were feeling rather tender down below but they honestly didn't care, as the waves of pleasure far overrode the pain.

When everyone had had their ride they released Ben and Dom who immediately turned to each other and kissed passionately. Cody and Sam helped them over to the red leather couch in the corner before returning to entertain the rest of the group. Now that they were left alone they cuddled up together on the couch, gently kissing and softly caressing each other's poor abused bodies.

Back on the stage, Eric, Adam and Steve were trying to handle all of Cody's amazing meat. Adam and Sam were working the shaft while Eric was nibbling on the hairless balls and letting his tongue stray underneath and between Cody's legs. Eric moved around to give Cody a very comprehensive rimming, before grabbing a condom and moving up to slam his cock into Cody's tight teenage ass, while Steve and Adam diligently continued to fellate him.

In the meantime, Sam was enjoying the attentions of Seb, Thomas and Andy. Thomas sat in the chair previously occupied by Ben and readied himself for Sam to ride him. Sam easily took Thomas' thick cock to base and bounced up and down for a few times before leaning forward and inviting Andy to shove his large, black cock inside him as well – a request that Andy readily accepted. No stranger to double penetration, Sam took it like a trooper as the two cocks slammed inside him and stretched him to his limits. Seb climbed up onto the chair and inserted himself in between Sam and Thomas so he was fucking Sam's face while being rimmed by Thomas. This sweaty combination worked rather well with all the participants enjoying the arrangement, especially Sam seeing he had three impressive pieces of meat currently invading his body.

Dom and Ben had sufficiently recovered from their earlier torture and were now fucking up against the wall. Ben was playing the role of the aggressive top, much to Dom's great delight. Steve and Adam broke away to play by themselves, with Adam being bent over the table and being ably fucked by his boyfriend. Steve was back in fine brutish form and seemed intent on claiming the tight ass as his alone by assaulting it with all his might.

After a while, Sam needed a bit of a break so he took leave of his playmates and moved over to where Cody was now forcefully fucking a very happy Eric. After watching for a few minutes he decided he wanted to plough his co-worker's ass, seeing he hadn't had it for a few weeks. Cody didn't skip a beat when he felt Sam's fat cockhead press against his slippery hole and simply shoved back to take the shaft in one go. Cody then skillfully rode his friend's cock while continuing to pound the ass in front of him.

Thomas was now sitting on the couch with Seb's face buried in his crotch, while Andy hammered into Seb's suntanned ass – there was nothing that Seb liked more than a good spit-roasting. Andy fucked him for a good ten minutes or so before wandering away to grab something to drink and rest for a spell. Seb wasn't too bothered and just moved forward so he could straddle Thomas, kissing him deeply as he felt the realtor's cock pushing up between his ass cheeks. Seb, ever the boy scout, reached over to the nearest pile of condoms and quickly prepared Thomas' member for entry into a not particularly exclusive club. Thomas slipped inside with ease and kept kissing Seb as he repeatedly slammed his horny hole.

As the evening wore on, the guests had played around in a myriad of combinations and positions and it all seemed to pass in a blur of kissing, rimming, sucking, fingering, licking and fucking. Luckily, Roberta always ensured that each of the special rooms was restocked every day with enough condoms and lube to keep a sauna going for a month. Time wasn't a problem because all the guys had chipped in to rent out the private lounge, and the charming company of Cody and Sam, for the entire night.

As night turned into day Dom and Ben once again became the center of attention as they were in the middle of the room fucking on the floor like savage animals. The rest of the guys reformed their earlier circle jerk, wanking over the muscular men as Dom relentlessly hammered Ben's aching ass. It was time for the last surprise, so Seb and Adam signaled to the group that it was now or never. They all picked up speed, determined to release their final gift as quickly as possible. It wasn't long before they started spurting, one right after the other, covering Ben and Dom from head to toe, with their cum dripping into every crease and crevice. Ben took this as his sign to blow and promptly add his own cream to the mix. Dom pulled out of his fiancé and let his seed fly as well, leaving them both a slick, sticky mess.

Cody and Sam then led the group, through a side door, to a large shower cubicle with three heads and adequate space for at least ten grown men to comfortably cleanup. They gratefully availed themselves of the facilities, taking care to help wash each other thoroughly. It was then that Seb sheepishly admitted to Ben and Dom that he'd orchestrated the spilling of the wine to enable them to strip the boys more easily. They broke into grins and revealed that they had suspected as much and easily forgave him his naughtiness.

Once they were all fresh and clean, they returned to the main room to dress and prepare to leave. Now that the lights had been turned up brighter they were a little confronted by the sight of the remnants of their passions – paper towels, empty condom wrappers and a tacky film of semen and sweat covering just about everything in sight. It was a good thing that the cleaners were used to such soirées and were well prepared to give the place a thorough cleansing after the room had been vacated.

They bid each other a fond farewell and departed back to their respective residences. When Dom and Ben eventually returned to their apartment, they climbed into bed and quickly fell asleep, content in the knowledge that they had amazing friends who would do anything to make them happy.

Brock's earlier prediction had come true with none of the guys, not even Dom, giving the disappearance of Dimitri a second thought until well into the following day. When Dom did manage to finally drag himself out of bed and come to think about it, he was very curious indeed as to what had happened to his wayward little brother...

WHITE CHOCOLATE VANILLA SPECULOOS CHEESECAKE

Ingredients:

2 eggs

1/4 cup sugar

1 teaspoon flour

1 cup white chocolate

1 & 3/4 cups Philadelphia cream cheese

1 cup milk

1 teaspoon cinnamon

1/2 cup crushed Speculoos biscuits

2 tablespoons of caramel essence

1/3 cup butter

Instructions:

Take note it is best to prepare the cheesecake the day before you plan on serving it.

Preheat oven to 180°C (350°F).

Grease a large round cake tin 18-20cm (7-8 inches) in diameter.

Melt the butter and mix it together with the crushed Speculoos biscuits and cinnamon in a large bowl.

Scoop the mixture into the cake tin and evenly cover the base.

Chill in the fridge for 20 minutes.

Melt the white chocolate and mix it together with the Philadelphia cream cheese, eggs, sugar, flour and caramel essence in another large bowl.

Remove the base from the fridge and pour the chocolate mixture evenly on top of it.

Bake for 35 minutes until the top is golden.

Leave on the counter to cool before placing it in the fridge to set for 12 hours.

Serve as desired.

SAVOURY VEGETABLE CAKE

Ingredients:

2 eggs

1 cup self-raising flour

1/2 cup milk

1 teaspoon olive oil

2 1/2 cups of chopped vegetables (mushrooms, broccoli, carrots, eggplant, capsicum, sweet potatoes…)

Instructions:

Preheat oven to 180°C (350°F).

Grease a cake loaf tin.

In a large bowl mix together the eggs, self-raising flour, milk and oil.

After it is well combined stir in the chopped vegetables.

(note if using harder root vegetables it is best to boil or steam them lightly beforehand so that they are partially cooked).

Pour mixture into the cake loaf tin.

Bake for 25-30 minutes or until golden brown.

Leave on the counter to cool for 10 minutes before serving.

KALUHA COOKIE SHOTS

Ingredients:

1 large egg yolk

2 cups flour

1/2 cup white sugar

1/2 cup brown sugar

1 cup Crisco

1 cup small chocolate chips

1 cup dark melting chocolate

1 1/2 cups of Kaluha

2 teaspoons vanilla extract

1/2 teaspoon salt

Instructions:

Grease a silicon popover mould.

In a large bowl combine the Crisco, brown and white sugars, egg yolk and vanilla extract.

Add the flour and salt, followed by the chocolate chips and mix well.

Put the mixture into the moulds making the sides of the shot about 1/2 cm (1/4 inch).

Chill in the fridge for 30 minutes before baking.

Preheat oven to 180°C (350°F).

Bake in the oven for 20 minutes until they start to brown.

Leave on the counter to cool.

Once cool, melt the dark cooking chocolate and pour into the cookie shots, coating the inside and the base.

Chill in the fridge until the chocolate has set.

Pour the Kaluha into each shot and serve.

HUSBANDLY DUTIES

Dom couldn't believe that the day he'd been dreaming about for so long was finally here. Surrounded by his nearest and dearest, he was the happiest he'd ever been in his life. He gazed lovingly into the beautiful brown eyes of his fiancé and said those magic words.

"Fuck me hard!"

Ben wasted no time in sliding his bare cock straight into Dom's waiting hole, as their friends stood around them, cocks in hand, anxiously awaiting their turn. All Dom could see looking up from his position in the sling was a circle of hard dicks attached to the beautiful bodies of his favorite playmates…Seb, Adam, Thomas, Steve, Eric, Andy, Max…they were all there to show just how much they cared.

Seb was closest to his head and promptly shoved his cock down Dom's eager throat, adding to the *pâtissier's* pleasure. As Ben pounded away, Dom reached up to run his hands over all those solid bodies and equally firm cocks. His moans echoed throughout the basement as he was pumped thoroughly at both ends. The basement of the café had gotten quite sticky and humid with all the man-on-man action and the men were soon slick with perspiration. It didn't take long for Ben to blow his sweet load deep inside the warm embrace of Dom's ass. He pulled out, his cock still dripping with cum, and moved aside for the next player.

Andy quickly took Ben's place and thrust his nine and a half inches of beautiful black meat straight inside, with Ben's cum acting as a most useful lubricant. Dom loved the feeling of Andy's raw cock filling his insides and stretching his passage. Ben then moved around and replaced Seb, so that Dom could lick his fiancé's cock clean. The other boys used their free hands to grasp and stroke Dom's muscular form, leaving no part unmolested.

Dom's slippery passage took Andy's cock with ease and it wasn't long before the familiar sensation of orgasm built up in Andy's balls and he too unloaded in his boss, his seed mixing together with Ben's. Andy slowly pulled out and wiped the excess cum off onto the entrance to further lubricate the hole for the next cock, before he moved around to have Dom lick him clean as well.

Thomas was the next in the queue and quickly took position at Dom's rosebud and proceeded to shove his unsheathed weapon into that tight Greek ass. He was extremely turned on knowing that his cock was being covered in a sticky mixture of Ben and Andy's cream. Thomas slammed into Dom again and again and could feel the ass contracting around his cock with every thrust. The way Dom was milking Thomas ensured that the realtor's cum was soon joining that of his friends and spurting deep inside.

The boys continued until each of them had delivered their creamy loads into Dom's well-ridden hole. Dom could feel the cum leaking out of his aching ass, some making its way underneath him and onto the sling, coating his lower back, while the rest dripped down to the increasingly tacky floor.

The last to unload in him was Seb, whose nine inches well and truly abused Dom's hole before releasing his precious seed inside him. After they'd done, they stood over Dom, wanking furiously as Dom pleasured himself. Dom was eagerly awaiting the shower of cum, desperately wanting to indulge his inner bukkake boy. He could see the guys beginning to tense up and just as the white shower of cum began to rain over him he sat up with a start.

"Fucking alarm." he cursed to himself as he quickly switched off the buzzer that had so rudely awoken him from his very pleasant, and rather wet, dream – judging by the sticky mess of precum he could feel on his stomach and cockhead. It was a shame that it hadn't been real, although the idea of setting up a sex dungeon in the basement of the café was an idea that had a certain appeal. Dom turned over and gazed lovingly at the sleeping man who he'd be marrying tomorrow. He gently stroked Ben's curly brown hair as he took in the beauty of his beau. The white cotton sheet had twisted to uncover Ben's bare bubble butt and Dom felt his natural urges kick in. The remnants of Dom's dream had left him in very aroused state, so using his precum, and a handful of spit rubbed at the entrance, he slowly maneuvered his cock into his sleeping fiancé's pale, round ass.

Ben slowly started to stir as Dom slid deeper and deeper inside the passage. Dom knew from experience that Ben loved being woken up by a gentle fucking, which always culminated in a thorough pounding once he was properly awake. Ben moaned softly and mumbled something inaudible as Dom picked up the pace. Dom could feel Ben pushing back into his crotch, which encouraged him to violate the velvety path with more vigor. Dom moved directly on top of Ben started really hammering him hard into the bed.

"Morning baby, that feels good." Ben said sleepily.

"You're telling me."

Given how worked up he still was from the debauched dream, it was only a few more minutes before Dom's body tensed up and he was depositing his seed deep inside his man.

When he was spent Dom collapsed down on top of Ben, a feeling that Ben would never tire of. They lay like that in contented bliss until Dom's cock began to soften and withdraw.

Dom sat up and let Ben turn over before swiftly moving downwards and practically inhaling the rigid unspent cock. He corkscrewed up and down the shaft, fondling the balls and letting his other hand tweak Ben's sensitive pink nipples. Dom's hand kept a hold of the balls, stretching them slightly as he let two fingers wander towards, and slip inside, the still sticky hole.

The re-penetration of his ass was the final straw and Ben was soon shooting his load into Dom's soft mouth. Ben's sphincter clamped down on the digits with each forceful spurt.

It was quite a big load, as was usually the case for Ben, and it leaked from Dom's full red lips and dribbled onto the white skin of Ben's defined stomach.

Once he gulped down the salty juice, Dom snuggled in close to Ben and lightly kissed the smooth skin of his neck and shoulders. They held each other tightly in their grand bed in the honeymoon suite, enjoying their post-coital bliss.

Unfortunately, they couldn't lie there all day, as much as they would have loved to. It was the day before their wedding and they still had a few things to do…like that big family brunch downstairs in a few hours. Although, as Ben felt Dom's cock begin to stir and poke into his side he thought that perhaps they had time for another play…or several.

* * *

Meanwhile in another part of the hotel Adam and Steve were cuddling in bed after an energetic morning fuck in the shower. They had been together for over six months now and they couldn't be happier. In fact, with all the excitement about the approaching wedding they had been seriously talking about moving in together. It would be a first for both of them and they were understandably nervous at the prospect.

Granted, it was rare that they actually spent a night apart these days but the next step on the road towards commitment was a daunting one, particularly for Steve who'd never had a real relationship before – well one that lasted more than a month at any rate. Despite their fifteen-year age gap they were rather well suited to one another, a sentiment shared by pretty much everyone that knew them.

Adam's parents had expressed a few doubts when he had first brought Steve home to meet them but they soon saw how happy he made their son and that his rugged exterior hid quite a loving man.

Laying there in bed together Steve could still feel the phantom sensation of his boyfriend's cock inside him – seeing he hadn't been particularly gentle in the shower – as well as the hot, thick, white load he had delivered inside him. He was glad that they had recently agreed to only use condoms for playtime with others. Steve loved being able to seed Adam's ass and have him return the favor, it made their sex feel more natural and unrestrained.... not that they were opposed to handcuffs on occasion.

They were half dozing, caught up in each other's arms, when they heard a knock at the door.

"Who could that be?" said Adam irritably, as he didn't want to be interrupted by anything.

"Probably just room service," replied Steve, "I ordered it before I jumped in the shower with you. Thought our morning exercise might give you an appetite." he joked.

"Well, you're right about that!" agreed Adam as he pulled Steve in for another passionate kiss.

Adam hopped up, quickly wrapped himself up in a big, fluffy hotel robe and opened the door. Standing at the door was an extremely handsome specimen of manhood, who looked to be in his mid-twenties. The waiter was tall, with piercing blue eyes and cropped brown hair, and his simple uniform of navy pants and a white button up shirt clung to him in all the right places. After Adam regained his composure, he stood aside to let him into the room.

"Where do you want it?" asked the waiter cheekily, giving a not so subtle wink.

"In the bedroom would be good," replied Adam, knowing that Steve was still laying naked in the bed.

The waiter smiled broadly as he wheeled in the trolley and saw Steve. The bulge in his pants started to grow even bigger when he caught sight off Steve's semi-hard cock starting to tent the silk sheets.

He lifted the lids off of the plates on the room service trolley, revealing their order of French raisin toast and pancakes.

"My name's Trent. Is there anything else I can do for you gentlemen?" asked the waiter while brazenly rubbing his crotch.

Adam answered by walking over, grabbing the waiter in a tight embrace and shoving his tongue into the pouting mouth. Trent kissed him back, grabbing at Adam's tight, toned ass through the robe. Adam then led the waiter to the bed, where Steve helped him in undoing the buttons and zipper before pulling off all his clothing.

"I was after a full room service," said Adam, just before taking Trent's pert right nipple in his mouth.

"Same here," said Steve, as he started roughly sucking on the other one.

Trent moaned as they teased and tormented his nipples. They pushed Trent down onto the bed and then worked their way down his ripped body until they came to his solid seven inches of mouth-watering manhood. Adam licked the head while Steve went straight for the balls, taking both and rolling them in his mouth while pulling away gently. Trent was reveling in the attention and was writhing on the bed as the dynamic duo devoured his crotch.

After a while Steve came up for air. He got up, went over to the room service trolley and grabbed the little jar of maple syrup that was sitting next to the pancakes. He brought it back to the bed and dripped it all over Trent's pale defined body, from his neck to toes. The boys then set about eating their 'breakfast'. Steve and Adam took their time, savoring each taste of the waiter, making sure that they licked him as clean as possible.

Trent was in no position to complain as he felt the mouths licking and biting, all up and down his body… not that he wanted to in the slightest.

When they had eaten away pretty much all the syrup, Steve gave Trent a passionate kiss before moving further up, straddling Trent's smooth and quite muscular chest and inserting his thick cock into the waiter's willing mouth. Trent eagerly took to his task, grabbing Steve's hips and pulled him forwards so he could take the cock deeper down his slick throat.

Adam moved downwards, tucked his shoulder-length red hair out of the way behind his ears, and spread Trent's legs up and out so that he could get better access to the tight opening he found between the firm buttocks. He started flicking his tongue across, teasing it, before beginning to probe deeper into the tempting passage.

Suddenly Steve broke away, stood up and grabbed some lube from beside the bed. His face fucking of Trent had given him an appetite for his boyfriend's alluring ass. Steve pulled Adam to the side of the bed and moved his throbbing cock up to Adam's hole and shoved it forcefully inside – only fair given the pounding Adam had inflicted upon his ass earlier. Trent seemed to take this as his cue, got up on his knees and began to fuck Adam's warm mouth.

Adam was elated as he was ploughed savagely on both sides, his own cock dripping precum all over the sheets. As the already frantic pace sped up further Adam thought he would pass out from the bliss. Adam never wanted them to stop but could feel the rhythm of the boys increasing and guessed correctly that he would soon be flooded with creamy cum.

The boys pounded even harder as their loads were about to spray. Steve and Trent came only a few seconds apart, spurting their hot seed into Adam.

Adam greedily guzzled down all of Trent's semen, as he felt Steve splashing his insides with his warm, sticky juice. He adored the feeling of being so full of cum and thought to himself that it was a shame he wasn't treated to such pleasure on a daily basis.

When they had finished unloading they both pulled out and lay beside Adam, resting a little.

"Now, what are we going to do about this?" asked Steve while grabbing a hold of Adam's throbbing cock.

" I think I can help with that." said Trent with lust in his eyes.

Trent leapt off the bed and grabbed his crumpled work trousers and extricated a condom packet from his pocket. He had been working there long enough to realize that the hotel was often frequented by handsome gentlemen of a certain persuasion, and knew it was always best to come prepared to accommodate any extra requests they might have.

Trent rejoined them on the bed, ripped open the packet and suited Adam up, before lubing himself and straddling the hot young man beneath him. Trent leant down to kiss Adam softly, tilting his hips back to spread his ass further open.

Adam pressed his cock against the waiting hole and pushed gently inside. Steve moved in behind Adam and helped him guide his cock into Trent's tight ass. Trent sat back so that Adam's cock slid right into the hilt.

"Fuck me hard boy!" grunted Trent.

Adam didn't need to be told twice and started pounding up, as hard as he could. Not wanting to be left out, Steve moved around in front of Trent, stood up on the bed so that his cock was at face level and pushed himself inside Trent's inviting mouth.

Adam had a spectacular view, looking straight up between his boyfriend's hairy, rock-solid legs up to his pendulous balls and seeing Trent's mouth working up and down the rapidly rehardening meat…truly a sight to behold.

Trent squeezed his ass muscles, trapping and releasing Adam's cock as it penetrated further inside him. At that moment Trent loved his job very much indeed.

Adam kept pummeling away, knowing that he wouldn't be able to last much longer so he sped up and really gave Trent a good seeing to. His cock slammed into the hole, over and over again, trying to invade deeper with every powerful thrust. Adam's hands were firmly on Trent's hips helping pull the waiter back down to be impaled on the stiff cock.

Trent could feel the cock inside him start to throb and was unsurprised when he heard Adam's gasps of pleasure mere moments later as he came inside the waiter's worked ass.

Steve was also ready to blow and happily shot a surprisingly thick amount, given his recent ejaculation, down Trent's accommodating throat.

Trent took himself in hand, and rapidly wanked until he blew a second load all over his own abs and cock. His cum dripped down through his short, dark pubic hair, over his smooth balls and onto Adam's flat stomach. Trent gingerly hopped off of Adam and lay beside him as Steve sunk back down to the bed as well.

They lay there recovering from their exertions for a while before Trent said "I should really get going, but thanks for that. Here's my number, give me a call when you guys need another playmate!"

"With pleasure," said Adam, with Steve nodding his approval. Trent then had a quick shower before getting dressed and leaving the boys alone once more.

"Looks like it's just you and me now Grizzly," said Adam. Steve smiled every time his young stallion of a boyfriend used this nickname.

"That's fine by me," whispered Steve as he gently brushed Adam's hair out of his face and pulled Adam towards him for another long, deep and passionate kiss….

* * *

Around the same time that Dom had been happily wrapped up in his dream, Seb and Thomas were heading down to the hotel pool. The two handsome blonds had been spending an awful lot of time together since the bachelor party. Thomas had been finding more and more reasons to drop by the café, and they had seen each other pretty much every day.

It was unusual for Seb to spend so much time with just the one man – he did so love to spread himself around…as many, many happy residents of the city could ably attest to – but they had clicked rather well during the celebrations and had found themselves drawn back to each other. Indeed, they were practically boyfriends, which to anyone knowing Seb's proclivities seemed to be a very strange state of affairs. Not that he was incapable of sustaining a relationship, in fact he had

had quite a few boyfriends, it was just that there hadn't been anyone that he'd cared for, beyond using them as a fun play toy, in quite some time.

Thomas was rather smitten as well and was quite content getting to know the handsome counter-hand inside and out. Not that he had been looking to settle down either, which is probably why they got along so well – that and the ridiculously hot chemistry between them whenever they were naked.

It hadn't really come as a shock to Dom or Ben when Seb checked into the hotel with Thomas. They knew their counter-hand's reputation well and to be honest were both secretly a little pleased that he had found someone to keep up with his desires.

Thomas and Seb took the elevator down from their 15th floor room and arrived into the spacious pool area that had a glass wall down one side, affording any swimming guests a magnificent view out over the harbor. They grabbed some large light-green towels from the pile by the door and dumped their belongings onto two sun lounges facing the window. They started undressing and quickly stripped down to their swimwear. Thomas was wearing a pair of short, fitted, blue swimming trunks that highlighted his full package and pert muscular ass. Seb had on his favorite pair of red swimmers that barely contained his man-sized cock and extremely fuckable ass, the sight of which appeared to make Thomas semi-hard straight away.

They jumped into the pool and splashed about having fun. Thomas decided to take advantage of the fact that they were the only ones there and grabbed Seb from behind, kissing the back of his neck while his muscular arms held him tight. Thomas' cock grew harder and rubbed up against the back of Seb's swimmers, seeming to want to poke through the material and into the firm, round ass.

Thomas spun Seb around so they were face to face and could kiss properly. Their hands roughly grabbed at each other's behinds. Thomas slipped his hands inside the swimmers and squeezed the round cheeks. He then spread Seb's ass a little wider and slipped a finger up against the ring. Thomas pushed against the hole, moving in a circular motion but without penetrating too far. Seb started to moan softly, so Thomas probed a bit more and pushed a second finger inside.

Seb pushed back against Thomas' hand, wanting to feel him further inside.

"Let's go somewhere a bit more private." suggested Thomas. They hopped out of the pool, grabbed their belongings, wrapped the towels around their dripping bodies and hurriedly went into the change room. Thomas dragged Seb into a changing cubicle and shut the door behind them. They dropped their towels and started fervently kissing and groping each other.

Seb couldn't wait any longer, so he ripped open Thomas' swimmers and eagerly gobbled down his cock. Thomas moaned and caressed the back of Seb's head as he slurped and sucked on that big, thick uncut cock.

Thomas loved the look of Seb's plump cocksucking lips wrapped around his member but he wanted them against his own. Thomas pulled Seb to his feet and pushed him against the side of the cubicle and kissed him deeply – his imposing Nordic frame easily holding the tanned surfer boy in tight to the wall. They continued moaning and grinding up against each other, enjoying the feel of each other's wet and slippery bodies.

Thomas spun Seb around to face the wall while he went to his knees, pulled down the back of Seb's tight swimmers and thrust his face deep inside the welcoming ass. Seb pushed back as Thomas hungrily rimmed him. Seb's cock was dripping precum all over the tiled cubicle floor as Thomas' tongue playfully probed inside him.

Both boys were moaning so much they hadn't heard someone come into the changing room. Suddenly the door to the cubicle was flung open. They were so shocked that they didn't even try to cover their rock-hard erections. The stranger was ruggedly good-looking, with a buzz cut, soft hazel eyes and smooth, tanned skin. He was wearing a tight white t-shirt that clung to his muscular torso and a pair of baggy yellow board shorts that showed the outline of one mighty piece of meat running down his leg.

"That's what I like to see, hot guys enjoying themselves!" he said with a grin. "That ass looks mighty tempting, mind if I have a taste?"

Before waiting for an answer the stranger sunk to his knees, spread Seb's cheeks wide open and shoved his face deep inside. Seb was still too shocked to resist but soon found his body responding automatically to the talented tongue.

Thomas saw how much Seb was enjoying it so decided to let the handsome stranger continue, while he moved down to sit on the floor in order to free the newcomer's cock from the board shorts. It was a little difficult at first, as the shorts were pulled tight against the delicious erection inside. Finally, Thomas freed the impressive uncut manhood and started sucking like he was dying of thirst.

The stranger devoured Seb's ass for a good five minutes before he pulled Thomas up from his cock and pushed him face first against the wall while pulling Seb down to the floor. He pulled down the back of Thomas' swimming trunks and opened the perfectly proportioned cheeks.

"How bout we share?" he said to Seb who enthusiastically agreed. Both of them started to eagerly eat Thomas' ass – licking, sucking, biting and taking turns to probe deep inside, working every last bit of the tight, sensitive hole.

Thomas was in heaven feeling the two mouths attacking his exposed entrance. He tilted his hips back so that the boys could feast as deeply as they wanted.

After a little while Seb and the stranger stood up, the three of them then started kissing, before they speedily removed the last bits of their clothing. Seb dragged Thomas back down to his knees and the two of them began to service the stranger's beautiful cock and balls.

The newcomer had a hand on the back of each of their heads, enjoying the sensatiom of those two sweet mouths pleasuring him. It wasn't long before the stranger started to tense up and the boys gathered that he was close to blowing, so they increased the intensity of their movements.

The stranger let out a little cry as he ejaculated and started to spray his load all over the waiting boys. Seb greedily lapped up as many spurts of sweet cum as he could while Thomas rubbed the rest of the spilt cream all over their faces and chests.

When he was finished the newcomer helped the boys to their feet and they started kissing again, their naked bodies slipping and sliding up against each other. The stranger could see that the boys' balls were heavy with creamy loads ready to spill.

"Let me help you out with those," offered the stranger.

He sunk to his knees once again and alternatively sucked Thomas and Seb's cocks, while he lightly fingered both their asses. The boys started to wank themselves as the newcomer moved down to sucking their balls, all the while probing their humid holes with his thick manly fingers.

A few minutes of this pleasure was all it took before they were both shooting their hot juice all over the handsome stranger's face and body. They pulled him up and let their cum mix together all over their moist bodies. After wiping each other down with the pool towels they sat down on the cubicle floor to rest.

"I'm James by the way, nice to meet you," said the stranger in a matter-of-fact manner.

"The pleasure is ours," replied Seb.

"Damn straight!" Thomas added.

The boys rested on the cubicle floor for a little while just chatting and caressing each other.

"How about a shower?" suggested James.

Seb and Thomas were amenable and the three of them gathered their clothes and made their way to the group shower area. They dumped their belongings on a nearby bench and turned on the taps. Since there was still no one around, they decided to share two corner showers so that their bodies were hit on both sides by the refreshing hot water.

They started to soap each other up as they moved together for a three-way kiss. Unsurprisingly, given the chemistry between the three, it was only a matter of minutes before all their cocks were once again erect and ready for action. James moved his hand down to Seb's ass and roughly shoved a finger inside.

Seb gasped with delight as he felt his hole being prodded and stretched. Thomas added to the fun by sliding one of his fingers into Seb's tight little hole as well. Seb's legs nearly gave out from the pleasure, so the boys held onto him tight as they both pushed their fingers in deeper, really probing his hot tanned ass. They turned Seb around to face the corner as they held him from behind, then sneakily slid in an extra finger each.

Seb grunted his approval as they worked his hole, all the while kissing and biting his back. Seb's long locks were plastered to his head as the water washed over him. He was pinned in by the muscular bodies and could only writhe in pleasure, as his cock practically gushed precum onto the floor. James reached around and grabbed Seb's cock with his free hand and starting jacking it rapidly.

Thomas joined in by grabbed Seb's large, smooth balls and pulling down lightly, knowing full well that it drove Seb wild.

The sounds of Seb's enjoyment were intensified by the tiled shower area and carried the noise out of the change room, where it attracted the attention of a hotel employee, Matt, who was passing by the pool to pick up the used towels. Matt recognized the noises for what they were – a man enjoying a great deal of pleasure. He stealthily wandered over to the change rooms, not wanting to disturb the fun that was being had. He pushed opened the door, realized that the moans were coming from the showers, so he slipped inside and peered around the corner. As soon as he saw the trio his pants tightened, his cock stiffening at the sight of the water glistening off of the fit bodies and the arousing activities they were engaged in. He quickly unbuckled his navy pants and took himself in hand, wanking slowly as he watched the men pleasure each other. They were totally oblivious to their audience as they continued to work their fingers inside Seb and playing with his cock and balls.

Matt watched them for a few minutes, completely entranced by the threesome until he suddenly realized that he was already supposed to be upstairs, helping to set up the dining room for a special brunch. Cursing his job under his breath he hastily zipped himself back up and beat a silent retreat, not wanting to have the guys' playtime stopped short as well.

Seb finally couldn't take any more, tensed up and starting spurting all over the white tiles. As the contractions in his ass stopped Thomas and James slid their fingers slowly back out. Seb turned around and the three men once more started kissing passionately and fondling each other.

"Maybe we should take this to my room for some proper fucking?" offered James. Seb and Thomas nodded in agreement, so the trio hastily got dressed again and headed out of the change room to continue their fun upstairs.

Unable to wait to get back to the room, they starting groping and kissing again as soon as the elevator doors closed behind them. They were like horny teens at a Christian summer camp – getting off on the sinful naughtiness of their actions.

James was grinding his hard cock against Seb from behind, while Thomas was in front of the pair doing the same. Seb adored being sandwiched and warmly encased by the two hunks. The elevator reached their floor and the boys managed to pull themselves away from each other long enough to make it to the door of James' hotel room and quickly get inside.

The boys were impressed with the room, which was almost the same size as their deluxe one but one floor down on the other side of the hotel, facing over the city.

"Let's get a bit more comfortable," said James as he grabbed their hands and led them towards the king-sized bed. James climbed on the bed, dragging Seb and Thomas behind him. Their clothes were off in record speed and soon they were all rolling around together, happily tasting each other and enjoying the feeling of all that naked flesh rubbing together.

James felt the need for cock in his mouth again and slid down the bed to start sucking on Seb's thick, juicy dick.

The boys soon followed suit with Seb moving around so he could gulp down Thomas' beautiful cock and Thomas in turn servicing James, forming a very hot daisy chain. While their mouths enthusiastically worked away their hands continued to roam…exploring, grabbing and squeezing the firmness of each other's well-built forms.

They worked each other's succulent meat like starved men, desperate to suck out the creamy treat within. Thomas moved around a little lower so that he had access to James' tight and inviting hole. First he licked, then he fingered, trying to open him up, much to the appreciative moans of James who was expertly chowing down on Seb's cock. Thomas then broke away leaving James to suck on the big cock firmly wedged in his mouth while he searched for a condom.

James guessed what he was after and pointed to the toiletry bag that was sitting on top of the dresser. Thomas found the stash of condoms and lube, and quickly rolled one on.

"Ready for that fucking now?" Thomas asked, already well assured of the answer.

James gave a muffled, yet enthusiastic, affirmative response, not wanting Seb's delicious cock to leave his mouth for a second.

Thomas took a handful of lubricant and covered his cock and the appealing entrance thoroughly. He started fingering James' hot little hole to prepare him for the nine inches about to invade it. James moved his hips; working his ass around the fingers, allowing them to go deeper and deeper.

After a few minutes Thomas decided to give James exactly what he was after and replaced his fingers with his thick cockhead and pushed inside.

James grunted as the cock first popped in then slid all the way to the base. He only needed a few seconds to adjust before he started working his hips and ass muscles once more, slowly milking the hard cock buried inside him, all the time continuing to do a most dedicated job of devouring Seb's manhood.

Thomas enjoyed James' skills but wanted to take back a bit of control so he slowly started pounding into the muscular buttocks, increasing his pace and intensity threefold.

On the other side, each thrust of Seb's cock seemed to go even deeper into James' throat but he took it like a trooper – which he had been until fairly recently, only leaving the Marines the previous year. In fact, that's where he had picked up a lot of his manhandling skills.

They kept this up for quite some time, James taking great delight in being hammered at both ends. Eventually he pried himself away from Seb's crotch long enough to demand that Seb join Thomas in ravaging his ass.

Seb swiftly sprang off the bed and grabbed some protection. Thomas pulled out, lay on his back on the bed and had James straddle him. James guided Thomas back inside him while Seb suited up. Seb quickly rejoined them and took his place straddling Thomas behind James. James leaned forward, allowing Thomas to half pull out so that they could he could accommodate them both. It took a little bit of effort, and a great deal of lube, but Seb started to slide in alongside Thomas. Their dicks pushed up against each other as they struggled to fit completely inside. Their labors soon paid off and James was full to bursting with cock.

James stayed still for a minute, savoring the feeling of being opened up by the two, almost identical, fat cocks.

"OK I'm ready," whispered James as he let the boys move around inside him.

They started off slowly, grinding more than thrusting, apparently wanting to stretch him out as much as possible before giving a proper pounding.

James leant forward and roughly kissed Thomas. Seb moved forward as well so he could lie down against James' back, compressing James between their two hot bodies. They soon became slick with perspiration, as they writhed together and the scent of their sex filled the air.

Seb sat back and started pumping into James with greater intensity, with Thomas soon following suit. James' breathing became labored as he struggled to take the massive amount of meat inside his aching ass. James made even more sounds of pleasure as the two cocks penetrated deep inside and spread his ass wonderfully, his moans and groans filling the hotel room.

The two blonds began to fuck James even faster and harder. Thomas grabbed a hold of James' cock, which was bouncing around in front of him and started wanking it rapidly. This had him to the point of ejaculation in just a few minutes. Without much warning he suddenly shot his load all over Thomas' chest as the boys kept battering away.

After James had finished blowing the boys slowly withdrew their still-hard cocks from his poor abused hole. They both removed their condoms and started jacking themselves furiously. In next to no time Seb was coating James' muscular back and ass with his sticky seed and Thomas was spurting all over his own solid chest. The three collapsed back down on each other, lying there in a warm embrace of sweaty, cum-covered skin and body heat.

After recovering from their manly exertions, they headed to the shower to wash off their fun. Unfortunately, Seb and Thomas had to be on their way to get ready for the brunch, so after they were freshly clean they politely made their excuses and thanked James for his hospitality. This worked out perfectly for Thomas as he had his own engagement to get to as well. They went in for another quick three-way kiss before leaving and promised to stay in contact for another bout of play in the hopefully not too distant future.

* * *

Around midday, the happy couple made their way down to the dining room for the pre-wedding brunch. They had invited their immediate family, who were all more than happy to attend. Dom's parents, Nick and Elodie, were there with his two older brothers and their wives and children. Dimitri, his little brother, hadn't yet made an appearance. Ben's parents, David and Ruth, had arrived with his sister Beth and her husband. Ben's other sister, Angela, was also there with her son, Dylan.

Sadly, neither of the couple still had living grandparents, who, despite being of an older generation, had been for the most part rather liberal and would have relished the chance to see their grandsons get hitched.

Ben's mother, Ruth, had always suspected that there had been more to the exceptionally close friendship of her son and Dom and wasn't surprised when they'd both come out and later began a romantic relationship. When they'd announced their engagement she couldn't have been happier, as she'd always thought of Dom as another son. Ruth was so pleased that she had started gently enquiring, at their engagement party, as to when they could be expecting some more grandchildren.

Their fathers had worked on the docks together for the last thirty years and their families had been entwined ever since. Of course, they had occasionally joked about some of their kids getting together but hadn't quite bargained on the eventual pairing.

In fact, both families had always been overwhelmingly supportive, although it was hardly as if Ben and Dom had been the first gay gentlemen in their respective families. Indeed, Ben's great uncle Flynn, whom he'd met a few times when he was little, had been of the same persuasion and had had a long-time partner who he'd sadly been unable to "officially" marry. It made Ben glad he lived in a more enlightened time.

Adam, Steve, Seb and Thomas ended up catching the same elevator down to the dining room, seeing they were staying on the same floor. Unsurprisingly, they were all in very good moods given their morning activities and the approaching weekend festivities. Andy and Max had been invited too but they had offered to keep the café open for the day so that it only had to close for a few days over the weekend. Dom and Ben very much appreciated their efforts and had planned to give them extra holiday days to repay their kindness.

Thomas and Seb were chatting with Ben, drinks in hand, when suddenly James walked into the room and came up and gave Ben a big hug and kiss on the cheek. Ben turned back to the boys and introduced James as his old college roommate who'd just moved to the city. Ben noticed the somewhat sheepish, embarrassed looks between the three of them and soon put one and two together to make threesome.

"You dirty little fuckers. That didn't take long, did it?" he joked with them and they all laughed breaking the awkwardness.

It was then that Dimitri walked in, accompanied by Jay – the stripper he'd met at Dom and Ben's bachelor party. Seb recognized him straight away and nearly choked on his Mimosa, but quickly recovered his composure. He hadn't realized that the duo would have kept seeing each other after the bachelor party. Seb had only arranged for the stripper to hook up with Dimitri and distract him from the deviancies he had planned for his brother, not for them to start dating.

It turned out that Dimitri and Jay had a lot more chemistry than just the sexual kind. Their drinks after the party had led to a sleepover, followed by several more catch-ups where they chatted as well as fucked liked oversexed teenagers. Dimitri learned that, far from being just a ditzy erotic dancer, Jay was actually studying medicine at the local university and had found that stripping was far more effective at paying off his student loans than a job at Starbucks.

Dimitri thought that Jay might baulk at the idea of being his "plus one" so early into their relationship but it felt like they had known each other far longer than just a few weeks. Indeed, both of them seemed quite smitten and had found themselves in the same unexpected position as Seb and Thomas…taken unawares by a relationship that involved more than just their creative use of their cocks on one another. Not to say that it hadn't been the driving reason for the initial attraction for both couples – one can't fight nature after all.

After introducing Jay to his family, Dimitri brought him over to Ben and the boys. Seb was momentarily confused when Dimitri introduced his companion as 'Jay' seeing as he had been going by the name of 'Brock' at the gentlemen's club - Stallions. Ever-adaptable Seb used the new name without missing a beat and didn't particularly feel the need to mention to Ben and Dom his role in Dimitri's new romance.

Dom and Dimitri's mother, Elodie, was impressed with the very handsome man her youngest son had brought along with him. She even asked Jay if he'd ever considered modeling. Now that her boys were all grown – and big boys they all were – she was starting up an agency using the contacts with whom she'd kept in touch.

Jay was flattered and told her that he'd consider it; it wasn't like he had an issue being treated like a piece of very edible meat, after all.

Seeing that all their guests had arrived, Dom and Ben started moving everybody over to the big, round table that had been set up for them. James sat himself next to Seb and Thomas so that they could continue chatting. The boys discovered that he was a former marine, had just moved to town and was looking for work as a personal trainer. Steve, who was seated a few places around the table, overheard the conversation and said that he was actually looking for some more trainers to fit into his gym's schedule.

Truth be told, Steve was always on the lookout for more talented eye-candy with which to fill his gym. He had to keep his clientele pleased after all and the fact that he insisted on a private session with every new trainer was something of a side benefit. Steve asked if James had time later that afternoon for an informal interview, to which James hastily replied in the affirmative. They organized to meet in the hotel lobby later that afternoon, both of them very much looking forward to it.

While Steve had been chatting to James, Adam had noticed that Trent was one of the waiters serving them. When Steve was finished Adam gave him a quick nudge in the side and discreetly pointed at the shapely server. Trent happened to look up at this point, gave them a quick wink and kept going about his business.

Matt was serving the omelets on the other side of the table and didn't realize that he had already seen some of the guests. It wasn't until he was directly behind Seb, looking at the back of their heads that a sense of familiarity started ticking away in his head. Just then Seb asked for one more plate and he instantly recognized the voice as belonging to one of the studs in the shower begging for more fingers in his abused ass. He nearly dropped the plate but pulled himself together and finished off the service.

As soon as Matt got back into the kitchen he couldn't wait to tell Trent about the hot scene he'd encountered earlier by the pool and that the participants were in the next room. Trent was rather amused and quickly filled in Matt about his morning romp with Steve and Adam. When they returned to the dining room the waiters repeatedly brushed up against the boys in question, not that any of them minded in the slightest. Truth be told, none of them were ever likely to be opposed to the attentions of handsome young men.

The conversations at the table tended to focus more on wedding related topics, naturally, including the impending tropical honeymoon the happy couple had planned with lots of sightseeing, sun baking and reading. They thought it best not to openly mention in front of their parents that the island in question was something of a notorious gay getaway and that there would doubtless be steamy sexcapades galore.

Once brunch was finished Dom and Ben headed off for a day of pampering while the best men, Adam and Seb, still had a few things to check up on. The others all went off on their separate merry ways, bidding each other farewell until the festivities the following day.

****

Knowing that Adam was going to be busy Steve decided to make the interview a more practical one and had James meet him in the hotel gym downstairs for an impromptu training session, so that he could judge his abilities in a professional capacity.

Steve walked in wearing a tight blue singlet and baggy red track pants that showed off his sizable meat, which was noticeably swinging from side to side as he walked. He had deliberately not worn underwear to see how James coped with distractions…among other reasons.

James was very impressed with Steve's bodybuilder form and openly admired the way his muscles strained against the singlet. James himself was wearing a loose black t-shirt and a pair of small green shorts that cradled his package rather nicely. He had noticed the way Steve had looked at the other men at the brunch and knew to play to his strengths.

"OK, show me what you got." Steve said with a smile.

James decided to run him through a fairly simple chest program, taking time to demonstrate all the appropriate stretches. Despite his attraction to Steve's manly frame and brute roughness he focused on the task at hand. As they trained, James told Steve about how he'd been a chubby child and a borderline obese teenager, so knew both the challenges involved in overcoming the physical and mental barriers to good health. His years of being taunted by schoolyard bullies had made him rather sensitive to the self-esteem issues clients faced. All in all, he was keen to make the world a happier, healthier and prettier place, one body at a time.

Steve was very impressed with James' honest, open manner as well as his technical proficiency when it came to training but given his ripped body the latter was hardly shocking. All qualities that Steve looked for in his trainers, that and how hot they were in exercise clothes… he did run a predominately gay establishment after all. Although, in all honesty he had found that the handful of straight men that trained at Sweat Station weren't opposed to the attentions of an experienced male mouth on their cock in the steam room from time to time.

Steve asked James how he felt about doing free programs for new members and doing the occasional floor-walking shift, helping out the men in need. James assured him he had no problems with that at all.

Their bodies started to glisten from their efforts, each man's muscles straining, as their clothes grew damp and began to give off a manly musk. They kept training as their chat moved on to the topic of James' time in the armed forces, Steve noticed that the former marine's crotch seemed to be growing bigger in his tight green gym shorts. Steve rubbed his own cock through the soft material of his track pants and was happy to see James' eyes go directly there. They kept chatting but the chemistry and heat building between the two was unmistakable.

James didn't want to make the first move seeing that this was his potential new boss but Steve quickly solved that problem by leaning forward, pinning James against the bench press with his solid build, and kissing him ferociously. James eagerly responded, running his hands over Steve's Herculean back and pulling the gym owner flatter against him.

Steve's cock was sticking straight up in his track pants, threatening to escape over the waistband, so he thought it was time to give it a helping hand. He stood up and brusquely pulled his pants down before grabbing James by the arm, jerking him up to a sitting position, then grasping the back of the trainer's head and forcing it down into his crotch.

James loved the ferocity of it as it reminded him of his first drill instructor. A nasty piece of work, but he was hot as hell and fucked like a demon…which James always took like a good little soldier. He had a feeling that today was going to be just as wonderfully nasty.

James soon showed Steve what he was made of and skillfully sucked the thick inches down his open throat. He could feel Steve's heavy balls banging against his chin and the thick black pubes rubbing against his nose as he endeavored to deep-throat Steve without gagging. The practice he'd had earlier that day on the thick monsters of Seb and Thomas certainly helped his technique.

After James had been sucking for a while, Steve decided to generously return the favor by squatting down, roughly removing the skimpy green shorts and devouring the thick cock he found waiting snugly inside. He played with the thick foreskin and pulled at it with his teeth, before moving down to savor the taste of the sweaty shaft.

From here Steve worked his way down and went to town on James' sweaty hole, lifting up the two muscular legs so he could get better access, shoving his face deep inside and letting his stubble rub away at the sensitive skin. He was extremely aroused by the taste of the salty, fragrant hole. Steve got up off his knees, went to the little gym bag he'd brought with him and grabbed some lube and condoms.

James gathered quite quickly that Steve had had this planned from the beginning, not that he was complaining. Once back Steve told him to stand up, which James promptly did, happy to be taking orders from such an angry top.

Steve bent him over the bench press, lined his cock up with the beckoning entrance and shoved himself inside violently.

James yelled out in pain and thought he was going to faint but quickly regained his senses when he realized that Steve would probably keep going anyway. After fucking him like this for some minutes, Steve pulled out and commanded James to lay on his back on the bench with his legs in the air.

When James was settled in position Steve wasted no time in slamming straight back inside the tender passage. Steve forced himself inside, not paying any attention to the grimaces of discomfort on James' face. Steve had his hands firmly pressing down on the smooth tanned chest beneath him, as he brutally penetrated James again and again. He raised his right hand up and repeatedly slapped James hard on the chest as he battered the beautiful buttocks underneath him.

While James was enjoying the harsh treatment, he was also happy that he would be spending that night alone to recover in peace. It had been a while since he was treated so roughly, and it was a good thing he'd had two big cocks up there earlier to loosen him up, otherwise he knew he'd be in a world of pain. Steve seemed to be fucking like he wanted to destroy his ass. Judging by the evil grin on Steve's face James guessed that he wasn't too far off the mark.

The mirror right next to them in the small gym started to fog up with the heat they were generating with their fucking. Sweat was dripping down off of Steve's hairy chest and onto James' smooth buff body.

Without warning Steve spat in James's face and demanded "You like that cum-whore?"

"Yes sir!" replied James with military precision.

Steve was enjoying the punishment he was inflicting but he also wanted to see his seed spread over James' face and chest, so he pulled out and tore off the condom. Then Steve straddled James' chest, pinning him to the bench as he wanked. James was still able to jack himself, as his arm was behind Steve's solid, furry thigh.

Steve only needed a few dozen stokes before he was blowing his creamy load over the former marine. It spurted directly onto his face and hair, running down his neck and shoulders. Steve shoved his still dripping cock into James' keen mouth to let him clean it up.

James kept jacking himself as he drained the last few drops from Steve's magnificent meat. He kept the cock in his mouth as he began to cum himself, sucking on it as he started to shoot his wad. He was so excited that it ended up spraying Steve fair in the middle of his back, where it mixed with the sweat and ran slowly downwards until it reached the curve of Steve's muscular buttocks and dripped down onto James' ripped six-pack.

Steve stood up and released James, pulled the personal trainer to his feet and kissed him hard again. Their sweaty cum-soaked bodies pressed up against each other. Steve licked some of his own cum off of James' face before he wiped off the rest with a towel. They picked up their clothes and walked into the little shower cubicles located just to the side. Fortunately, they could clean up without encountering any staff.

Once they were all freshly washed and clean again, Steve came over and slapped James hard on the ass and said. "You're hired! But we will probably need to do monthly checks to re-evaluate your performance."

James just smiled. "I'd prefer weekly actually, if you don't mind."

Steve slapped his ass again, pushed him up against the wall and kissed him hard.

When they broke for air he replied "I'm sure something can be arranged".

They finished dressing, said their goodbyes and returned to their respective rooms. James was walking with a tender gait as he entered the bedroom of his suite, eager for a good rest after such a thorough workout. Climbing into bed for a quick nap, as he started to drift off he thought to himself, that as far as job interviews went, he couldn't have asked for any better.

* * *

After one last meeting with Charlotte to make sure everything was going according to plan, Ben and Dom headed down to the hotel spa for their complimentary couples' massage. They had also booked themselves in for a variety of other treatments – facials, manicures, wraps and the like – to help relieve their stress and to look their very best for the big day.

Upon arriving at the spa they were given comfortable, white, oversized robes and shown to the lockers, so they could strip off completely before the massage. When they were ready, the lovely lass at reception led them into a large room with dim lighting and soft new-age music playing through the speakers overhead.

They disrobed and laid face down on the benches and soon had strong, oiled-up Swedish hands attacking their knotted muscles with brute force. Normally such vigorous treatment of their bodies would have excited the boys but seeing the hands in question belonged to two sturdy middle-aged Swedish sisters there was little chance of any unwelcome erections. The soothing music and the unlocking of their muscles soon had them drifting off slightly. It was, however, slightly different to the last massage they had had together with their buff neighbors, Tom and Finn, from downstairs. Sure there had been a lot of oil, and strained muscles but the deep tissue manipulation had been mostly internal and it hadn't been a strictly professional arrangement.

They'd originally, informally, met them when they were first checking out their new apartment and had seen them fucking on the balcony below theirs. After running into them a few times at the pool in the courtyard of their apartment complex, they had invited them over for dinner. They passed a pleasant enough meal together but their dessert – pistachio ice-cream with an apple tart – ended up being eaten off of each other on the terrace… followed by a dedicated effort on all parts to stretch and strain each other's bodies until they were completely relaxed. It had been a somewhat sticky but very enjoyable end to their evening indeed. They had played with their neighbors a number of times since then and were looking forward to catching up with them again after their honeymoon.

The beauticians were quite thorough in their work. Indeed, their bodies hadn't been prodded, poked and rubbed so hard since that week they'd spent in Berlin the previous year. Although, come to think of it, they had ended up a lot dirtier by the end instead of the pristine sparkling clean they were aiming for this time round.

Once done, they practically drifted back up to their room in a haze of blissful contentment and prepared to have a peaceful evening in their hotel room, happily wrapped up in each other's arms.

* * *

While Steve had been putting James through his paces, Seb and Adam had gone upstairs to put together the centerpieces and make sure that all the place cards were in the correct order, lest there be any unfortunate pairings on the day. This left the threesome of Dimitri, Jay and Thomas to amuse themselves, so they decided to hang by the outdoor pool to sun bake and frolic for the afternoon.

It was wonderful weather for it and, fortunately for the boys, there were quite a number of handsome gentlemen in skimpy swimwear that had had the same idea. The trio had a most marvelous time taking in the view, relaxing and chatting about nothing in particular.

After a few hours Seb joined them on the pool deck, as he wanted a break before completing the last chore of picking up the wedding cupcakes that Andy had made earlier that day from the café.

Meanwhile Adam had gone off to find Steve, eager for some more intimate time, and keen to know how the interview with James had gone. Although he had a pretty good idea that it would have ended in sweaty man-on-man shenanigans...his boyfriend could be a little predictable at times – especially when it came to eager men with hard bodies.

The foursome splashed about in the pool until the early evening when Seb announced that he really must go to do the pickup. The boys offered to go with him to help, figuring it would take them a lot less time if they all assisted with the packing and transport.

They took the café delivery van that Adam had left in the hotel parking lot. Seb was driving so Thomas hopped in beside him, while Dimitri and Jay climbed in the back. It would be a cozy fit on the way back loaded up with cupcakes but it was hardly as if the boys were averse to being in close company.

When the boys arrived Seb instructed Thomas and Jay to start unloading the cupcakes from the walk-in cooler while he and Dimitri went downstairs to fetch and fold some boxes to put them in. Once they were in the basement all alone, Dimitri cornered Seb and said "Jay told me what you arranged at the bachelor party."

Seb was a little nervous, as he'd been worried that Jay would spill the beans and wasn't sure how

Dimitri would react to the news that he'd been set up.

"I've only got one thing to say, you conniving little slut!" Dimitri said as he lunged forward and pushed Seb roughly up against the wall. He moved his face forward right up to Seb's then gave him a deep passionate kiss, which was the last thing Seb expected but he took no time in responding back in kind.

Dimitri pulled away, grinned and said "Thanks. He's been the best thing that's happened to me in a while."

Seb smiled, glad that he had been forgiven and that his actions had lead to an unexpectedly pleasant coupling for all concerned. He took the opportunity to kiss Dimitri again, which was enthusiastically reciprocated. Their hands started roaming, pulling at each other's clothes and rubbing the hard bodies beneath through the material, neither of them apparently caring that the men they were dating were in the kitchen above them.

Seb's hands began undoing the button fly of Dimitri's jeans, and soon he had his hands on the delicious Greek meat that was leaking precum like a tap. Seb hastily sunk to his knees and began to give the cock the attention it deserved. Seb pushed the jeans and red underwear down further so he could have full access to the thick, juicy cock and heavy, hairy balls. Using one hand to work the shaft and the other to fondle and tug on the ball sack, Seb was giving Dimitri the very best of his expertise.

Dimitri had wanted to get his hands on – and cock in – Seb for quite some time, ever since he first popped into the café to check out his brother's business. Seb's flirtatious manner had caught his attention and he wanted a taste. Dimitri grabbed Seb by the back of the head, his fingers grabbing a hold of that long blond surfer-hair and started fucking the counter-hand's wet mouth.

It was then that Jay and Thomas decided to come downstairs to see what exactly was taking the boys so long. They were about midway down the stairs when they saw Seb on his knees with a throat-full of thick cock. Neither of the boys seemed particularly surprised or even unhappy to see their paramours in such a compromising position. Seb and Dimitri had noticed the entry of their companions but didn't let that slow them down in the slightest.

When they reached the bottom of the stairs Jay and Thomas did what any self-respecting man would and simply started to play with each other – besides they had been quite unashamedly admiring each other since brunch. Soon they, too, had shorts unbuttoned and unzipped, cocks out and in hand. Trying to keep pace with their promiscuous boyfriends, they progressed fairly rapidly from kissing and groping to sucking and fingering.

Thomas went down on Jay first, valiantly attempting to choke down all that delicious cock; it took some effort and his eyes were watering but he got down to the base, loving the feeling of the thick cock wedged in his tight throat. He corkscrewed up and down the cock trying to deep-throat as much as he could without cutting off his air supply completely.

Jay was very appreciative of the effort and gently encouraged Thomas with his hands slightly stroking the realtor's soft blonde hair as he went about his task. Jay locked eyes with Dimitri as they both fucked the faces of the willing boys in front of them.

Jay wanted to share the pleasure and pulled Thomas down onto the floor, pulling off the rest of their clothes as they went, before launching themselves into a very intense sixty-nine.

By this time Dimitri had Seb pushed up against the wall and was giving his beautiful tanned round ass a meticulous rimming. His big strong hands spread the cheeks wide and allowed Dimitri to push his face deep inside the tasty tunnel, savoring every bit he could stick his tongue into. Dimitri then spun Seb around and dived down on the nine inches of mouth-watering manhood in front of his face. To be honest, with all the practice he'd been getting with Jay's ten inches he had become quite adept at taking larger appendages in both ends.

Jay swiveled around so that he was face to face with Thomas then they began kissing again, their hands running up and down, fingers going into creases and prying wherever they could. Thomas loved the feel of Jay's smooth skin pressed up against his, and their kisses became very fiery and passionate. The contrast of Thomas' pale skin against that of Jay's darker Eurasian hue was quite something to behold. Thomas' fingers found the crease of Jay's beautiful toned ass and went exploring in between the cheeks.

Jay relaxed his hole so that Thomas could shove his thick fingers inside him. He was gentle at first but Jay's increasingly loud moans of appreciation encouraged him in his endeavors and he soon had two fingers in well past the knuckles.

"Fuck me Thor," Jay joked, making fun of Thomas' Nordic looks. Not one to leave a man in need, Thomas got up and went over to the big, brown box of condoms and lube, which was on sitting in the bottom corner of the shelving under the stairs.

A few months beforehand the boys had unanimously decided at a staff meeting that they would all contribute to having a well-stocked store of such supplies on hand should the need arise. This was quite a sensible idea really, given the high sex drives of the staff and the times the café had been used as an unofficial sex-on-premises venue. Honestly, sometimes it seemed busier than ManHole - the number one sex club in town.

Jay moved onto his back, lifted his legs up and spread them wide. His years of stripping had made him extremely flexible and he certainly knew how to put on a show.

Thomas dropped back to his knees, ready and raring to go. He penetrated Jay again, this time with fingers thoroughly coated in lube and worked Jay's hot, hairless hole for a minute or two before placing his cockhead at the entrance. Thomas directed his cock just inside, going slowly to allow Jay to adjust.

Jay wasn't known for his patience and grabbed Thomas by the hips and sharply pulled him forward, ensuring he was immediately full of rock-hard cock. When he felt Thomas' pubes against his balls he let out a sigh of contentment and let Thomas start pounding away.

Dimitri had gotten to his feet once again and was kissing Seb passionately against the wall. They were so engaged in their play that they didn't notice their partners had started fucking in earnest until they heard Jay begging for Thomas to really pound his ass, followed by the severe slapping of skin and Jay's moans on enjoyment.

"I think we should catch up," said Dimitri with a cheeky grin.

"My thoughts exactly," replied Seb.

They quickly discarded the rest of their clothes and Seb went to the same box in the corner and grabbed the necessary equipment. He walked back to Dimitri as he ripped open the condom packet and slipped the latex onto Dimitri's erect cock in one fluid motion – he had had quite a lot of experience. Seb smeared lube on the cock and into his own hole before bracing himself up against the wall, tilting his hips back to give Dimitri open access. Dimitri lined himself up and then proceeded to violate the counter-hand's velvety passage, one inch at a time. Seb was still tight, despite his morning's play, but it didn't take him long to adjust to the solid piece of meat inside him and was soon pushing back into Dimitri's increasingly forceful thrusts.

The basement echoed with sounds of male bonding – sweaty skin slamming together, moans of enjoyment and the occasional grunts of encouragement.

Thomas wanted to switch it up so he pulled out, told Jay to get on his knees and then took him from behind, with both of them facing the other couple fucking against the wall.

"Fuck him harder! He can take it!" Thomas called over to Dimitri, as he continued ramming into Jay's sensational ass.

Seb looked over his shoulder and poked out his tongue at Thomas but enjoyed the increased force which Dimitri was now using on his ass. This continued on for some time but eventually Seb had to beg for a break, his well-ridden butt needed a slight reprieve. Dimitri pulled out, whipped off the condom, turned Seb around and kissed him deeply again. They broke away and then decided to join the other two in the middle of the floor.

Meanwhile, Jay and Thomas had decided to swap positions and it was now Thomas on his hands and knees being violated from behind. Jay, however, was taking it easy due to his length being something to get used to, so he was slowly opening Thomas up more before going in for a truly forceful fucking.

Dimitri had an idea, promptly got on the floor on his back and inched himself underneath Thomas until he was at crotch level and started sucking the realtor's cock, draining the delicious precum that was leaking from his juicy cockhead.

With Dimitri's thick meat in his face Thomas knew exactly what to do and started pleasuring it with his mouth.

Seb had his own ideas on how to complete the tasty tableau and went back to the stockpile to get himself suited himself up. When he came back to the boys he got on his knees and proceeded to spread Dimitri's legs, gave the newly exposed hole a hasty rimming then slipped his cock deep inside.

Dimitri gave a loud grunt of appreciation as Seb's cock slid in him all the way to the base but kept working Thomas' meat like a professional.

As they pumped away into the two willing asses before them, Jay and Seb leaned forward and kissed over the two bottoming boys. They fucked hard and fast, egging each other on while the two men in the middle accepted the punishment of their holes without objection. Granted it would've been hard to understand anything they said seeing they both had mouths full of cock, but past history had shown that they were both more than capable of taking such assaults on their holes.

After a solid fifteen minutes of such enthusiastic fucking all four fit bodies were slick with sweat. Jay was keen to try something new so he pulled out of Thomas, swapped condoms and went around behind Seb and shoved himself inside the already lubed passage.

Seb had a sharp intake of breath as all ten inches penetrated him at once. True to form, he paused only briefly before continuing to plough Dimitri and squeezing his sphincter to try to control the thrusts of the intruder inside him.

Jay was happy to let Seb work his dick and was very impressed with the counter-hand's muscle control. He had met so many guys that simply didn't know how to use their asses properly and just took his massive meat lying there like a starfish. Jay sometimes seriously thought about setting up some sort of sex school to try and educate these poor men and make the world a better place one power bottom at a time. Fortunately, Dimitri was not in need of such training and Jay was very satisfied with the way his boyfriend handled his almost daily penetrations.

Thomas decided he wanted to top again, seeing that his ass was now unattended, so he pulled away from Dimitri's delicious dick and talented mouth and went to get fresh protection. When he got back he motioned to Seb that he wanted his turn fucking Dimitri, so Seb graciously pulled out and let Thomas take his place.

Dimitri took the new cock with ease – no doubt helped by the fact that Seb and Thomas were near identical in thickness and length. Dimitri was soon demanding that Thomas plough him harder, which Thomas was more than happy to accommodate.

Jay then spun Seb around and onto his side, all the while keeping inside him. Seb cried out as Jay's huge cock turned inside him, stretching him. Jay was still on his knees and penetrating him in a horizontal direction, which probed Seb at a very pleasant angle. Seb was finding it difficult to think as the waves of pleasure washed over him with each thrust.

Jay bent over to kiss Seb fervently as he penetrated him with quick, short jabs.

Next to them Thomas and Dimitri were also kissing as Thomas had changed from the brutal pounding to long-dicking – slowly sliding himself all the way in and almost all the way out of Dimitri's abused ass.

The foursome fucked like this for some time, enjoying the fun of their partner swapping games. After a while, Jay and Thomas both pulled out and decided to finish off, so they could all get back to the task they had originally come to do. The boys got to their feet and moved together to form a circle jerk in the middle of the floor. Their free hands wandering over each other – tweaking nipples and squeezing balls – to help get each other off.

It was at this opportune time that Adam appeared at the top of the stairs. He had been quickly dropping by to pick up his wallet that he absent-mindedly left there the previous day, when he saw the basement door open and had heard of the sounds of sex. Curious, and horny, he ventured downstairs and was greeted by the site of the foursome in action and close to orgasm. Adam quickly cast aside his t-shirt and cargo shorts and walked right up to the boys and asked if they had room for one more.

After recovering from the surprise of the unexpected visitor, they stepped aside and let him into the middle.

Adam quickly sank to his knees and was faced with veritable banquet of manhood. He set to work, tasting all the cocks and balls, spending only a minute of two on each, trying to please all of them the best he could. The boys looked down in appreciation of his efforts, in between rounds of kissing each other.

The loads had been building in their balls for about an hour, so it didn't take much of Adam's stimulation before they were ready to blow. They jacked themselves while Adam continued to nibble and fondle their balls. It only took a few minutes before they started erupting one right after the other. Adam kept at his work as the salty-sweet cream rained down upon his pale skin and long red hair.

When they were done they pulled Adam to his feet and played with his body, licking each other's cum off of the dirty delivery boy. Adam wanked himself furiously as he could feel all those mouths and hands attacking his body – pulling at his balls, probing his hole and biting his neck. A few moments later Adam was spurting his own load all over the basement floor, adding to the sticky mess that had dripped of his body.

Seb went and got some paper towels so that they could clean themselves up. They wiped each other off, laughing and joking as they went, stopping to give the occasional kiss or slap across a bare ass. When they were done, the boys put their clothes back on and headed back upstairs with the boxes. It was starting to get late, so they swiftly packed up the cupcakes, loaded the van and headed back to the hotel.

The café had seen quite a lot of action over the past few years but the fivesome in the basement was perhaps the hottest so far.

* * *

Much later that evening, Matt was in the kitchen putting away some dishes on a high shelf in the kitchen when he shifted his weight at the wrong moment and the stepladder he was on gave a sharp lurch to the right. He tumbled down, dropping plates and banging into a box that was sitting on the counter before coming to rest on the floor. Matt quickly took stock of himself and realized that he only had a few bumps, and no doubt bruises, but was otherwise alright. He was thankful that no one else had been in the kitchen to observe his clumsiness. It was only when he looked around him to survey the damage that he realized the extent of his accident. Aside from the shattered plates and scattered jars, the box that he'd hit on the way down had skidded across the counter and fallen on top of the wedding cake, which had been sitting on a low trolley. He'd actually been the one to take it out of the walk-in cooler minutes earlier when he'd been rearranging the boxes.

Matt could see that the top tier was completely ruined and possibly the level below as well. After swearing and sweating for a few good minutes he knew that he'd have to tell the happy couple about the unfortunate accident. He was on his way to the elevators when he caught sight of Andy, who he'd seen helping deliver the cake earlier that day. Andy was there to drop off some insurance papers for the café that Dom and Ben had forgotten to sign with all the activity in the lead up to the wedding. He immediately saw that Matt was in a bit of a state.

Desperately afraid that he'd lose his job over it, Matt told Andy what had happened and then took him back to the kitchen to see the catastrophe. Andy assessed the damage and was able to tell a very relieved Matt that the second tier was salvageable but that he'd have to make a new top layer.

Andy instructed Matt that Dom wasn't to know, as he didn't want to ruin the happy couple's night. Fortunately, the hotel kitchen was extremely well stocked and he had all the necessary ingredients on hand to make a new tier and redo the icing. In another stroke of luck the cake topper of two grooms – miniatures of Ben and Dom that one of their talented sculptor friends had been able to make for them – had only been knocked aside and was still intact.

"I'm going to need your help and it's going to take a while, so I hope you don't have any plans." Andy said to the grateful waiter.

"Anything you need," replied Matt. His shift was just about to end so he had more than enough time to spare. Now that his terror of being fired was gone he was able to appreciate the beautiful black man beside him.

Andy had Matt measure out the ingredients as he started making the cake mix. Andy got to work straight away and with the very repentant boy helping out they had the cake cooking in no time. While it was in the oven, Andy prepared the icing while Matt cut up the red fruits that were going to be used for decoration. They chatted while they worked, with Matt telling the *pâtissier* about his plans for when he finished college – he was studying to be a marine biologist – and Andy told him about his passion for food and how he hoped to one day have a shop of his very own.

Once the cake was cooked, Andy took it out and left it to cool on the counter while he helped Matt clean up the rest of the mess caused by his fall. By the time everything was back in place, the cake was cool enough to add the decoration. Matt stood in awe as he watched Andy's nimble fingers smooth on the icing and deftly place the fruit around the edges. When Andy put the cake topper back where it belonged Matt breathed a huge sigh of relief and was ever so thankful for all of Andy's help.

They put the cake back on the trolley and rolled it into the cool room. After they had washed up the bowls and utensils they'd used, Matt asked Andy if there was anything else he could do to make it up to him. Andy replied by pushing Matt down to his knees, grabbed him by his spiky-haired head and shoved his crotch in Matt's startled face.

Matt didn't need any further instruction and quickly pulled down Andy's zipper and helped himself to the rapidly hardening cock he found inside. Matt worked the shaft like a champ, although he began to gag a little when Andy became fully erect and over nine inches of thick black meat filled his mouth and throat. He undid Andy's pants further and pulled them down around Andy's ankles, as he made a valiant effort to suck down on the big cock and smooth balls. Matt ran his hands all over Andy's muscular black legs while wanking that succulent meat, kissing and licking all around his crotch.

Andy yanked Matt up to his feet, pushed him up against the counter and kissed him fervently. He reached down and roughly ripped open Matt's navy work pants.

Andy wanted a taste of Matt's cock and dropped to his knees to devour Matt's delicious dick.

Matt grabbed the back of Andy's head pulling him in close as his thick seven-inch cock went further down the *pâtissier's* throat. Matt liked the feeling of running his hands over the rough texture of Andy's cropped hair as Andy ravenously consumed his cock and balls. He felt the long tongue teasing all over his shaft and under his balls working closer to his ass.

Andy then spun Matt around bent him over the counter and started to rim his cute little butt. As Matt bent further over the bench his work shirt lifted up and Andy could see that he had a tattoo of a star with the longest point at the bottom looking like an arrow pointing towards a heavenly ride – a tramp stamp if ever there was one.

Andy licked it as he stood up and grabbed the bowl of leftover strawberries sitting on the bench. He kissed Matt on the back of the neck before squatting back down.

"Spread your ass boy!" he commanded and Matt swiftly obeyed using to his hands to spread his cheeks nice and wide. Andy picked up the strawberries and started pushing them inside the tight hole, one after the other.

Matt squirmed as he could feel the fruit popping inside him, unsure of where this encounter was headed but loving every second of it. He was almost glad that he'd fallen off that ladder if this was his karmic reward.

The red juice from the strawberries starting running down Matt's lean toned legs as they were squashed together inside his tight passage. After Andy had squeezed all the fruit inside, he shoved his face deep inside to start eating them back out again. Andy placed his hands on top of Matt's and used them to spread the ass cheeks even wider.

Matt felt a twinge of discomfort as he was stretched but that was soon forgotten as soon as he felt Andy's soft tongue penetrating even deeper. Matt was wriggling in pleasure, up on his toes, as he felt Andy ruthlessly raiding his ass with the tongue in the desperate search for every last piece of sweet fruit.

When Andy was satisfied that he had thoroughly cleaned the boy out, he moved back and started licking and biting the toned buttocks, moving under and licking the waiter's low-hanging balls. Andy then kissed his way up and down Matt's legs, licking up the juice that had drizzled down them.

Andy slowly made his way up and pulled Matt back up off the bench to a standing position. He started to undo the buttons of Matt's white work shirt from behind and when it was open Andy ran his hands over the tight, toned body, from the defined eight-pack of his stomach, all the way up to his firm, compact pecs.

Matt could feel Andy's cock rub slowly against his crack, grinding gently as the *pâtissier* kissed his neck and nibbled on his ears. Matt pushed back against the solid dick and felt it slide in between his cheeks and come to rest against his sticky, moist hole. They stayed like this for a little while, apparently enjoying the firmness of each other and the body heat that was being generated between them.

As pleasant as this was, Andy wanted more – namely to be balls-deep in those cute buns. Andy quickly took off the rest of his clothes and told Matt to do the same. They were soon both standing buck naked in the kitchen and ready for more play.

Andy had done a marvelous job preparing Matt's hole for his planned invasion but he wasn't finished yet. To loosen the young waiter up further he grabbed the leftover butter and a white plastic rolling pin lying nearby – he didn't want the boy to get splinters from a wooden one, after all. It was about ten inches long, with smaller plastic handles on either side. Andy bent Matt over the counter again, greased the left handle of the rolling pin with butter and slid it into the moist entrance. The handle went in easy enough but Andy had to work the hole a bit, moving the rolling pin in circular motions while pushing until Matt's sphincter relaxed and took it further inside. Andy managed to get a good two-thirds of it inside Matt who was grunting and groaning as the pin stretched him in all manner of different directions.

At twenty three years of age, Matt was hardly a virgin and the rolling pin, while very fulfilling, wasn't a good enough substitute to satisfy his carnal urges for the real thing and he was soon begging for Andy's chocolate meat to be inside him. Handily, Matt had a condom in his wallet, so he hopped off the rolling pin, grabbed the rubber and gave it to Andy. Andy rolled it on, grabbed some more butter for lubrication and to push his way inside that still rather tight ring. He started off gently but Matt demanded to be fucked roughly so Andy obliged and was surprised by how much the boy could take.

Andy slammed his large cock into Matt's slick passage again and again, causing the waiter to moan louder and cry out in appreciation. Matt lifted up one leg and put his foot on a nearby box, allowing Andy deeper access inside. Andy ploughed him hard, with Matt enjoying every last inch. He had a thing for darker guys and Andy was certainly hitting the spot. Fortunately it was rather late at night by this time and the sound of their fucking – like wild animals in heat – wasn't overheard by anyone. It wouldn't have done for him to almost lose his job again.

Sadly, all good things must come to an end and this was no different. After about thirty minutes of pounding over various counters and on the floor both boys were in need of release.

Andy was on his back on the floor and Matt was straddling him, riding him like a bucking bronco. Andy's hands were firmly on Matt's hips as he bounced up and down on the big black beast within him. Matt was wanking furiously, his hand practically a blur as it worked his shaft hard and fast. Andy could feel the boy tensing up so pounded upwards and was rewarded with the sight of Matt throwing his head back as he ejaculated. The white creamy load spewed forth from his rock-solid cock and all over Andy's beautiful black chest.

The contraction of Matt's ass on his cock and the sight of the boy in such ecstasy was almost overwhelming for Andy who felt the load in his balls about to erupt through his cock. He lifted Matt off of his cock, ripped off the condom and only needed one or two strokes before he was shooting all over himself. When he had finally stopped spurting he pulled Matt down to him where they kissed, as their cum rubbed together between the sweaty bodies and dripped down onto the floor. They stayed there on the floor for quite a while just kissing, Andy's hands cupping Matt's well-worked ass while Matt gently stroked Andy's head.

Matt could have happily stayed like that for hours but he knew he had to re-clean the kitchen and then get home if he wanted to get enough sleep before work tomorrow.

They reluctantly got up off of the messy floor with Andy helping Matt with the clean up. Four hands are better than two – in just about every situation really. They parted ways after a few more deeply passionate kisses, both unwilling to finish their playtime.

After he had finally left Matt, Andy remembered the papers but he realized it was far too late to drop them upstairs. He decided to leave them in an envelope at reception, which Dom would be able to pick up tomorrow when he got a chance. That done, he made his way downstairs to the car park so he too could head home and grab some much needed rest before the big day.

* * *

While Andy and Matt had been working in the kitchen, Ben and Dom were relaxing on the sofa in the honeymoon suite. They were watching a big, dumb action film, that didn't have much in the way of and script or acting but was heavy on special effects and gratuitous half-naked shots of the buff male stars so the boys were happy. About halfway through the film there was a knock on the door. They just assumed it was the room service they had ordered earlier and were slightly surprised but pleased nonetheless to discover Jonathan waiting there. Ben then remembered that he had asked Jonathan to drop by to give them a quick listen to the set he had planned for tomorrow. Ben apologized for his silly lapse of memory and they welcomed him inside.

A few minutes later there was another knock on the door, which was the room service this time, with a bottle of champagne and some nibbles. They offered Jonathan a glass and some food while they started listening to the set. As the music played they chatted about old times, when they used to all go out clubbing together, staying out all night dancing and messing around with boys. Time flew and they ordered another bottle of champagne – that Jonathan insisted on paying for – which was delivered promptly and opened with glee. After a few more glasses the champagne had had the desired effect and the three of them were more than a little tipsy and up and dancing around the lounge room of the suite. Jonathan's floppy brown hair was flying all over the place as he drunkenly bounced around to the music. The dancing was sweaty work and soon their t-shirts were lying on the floor as they continued on in their revelry.

The boys moved in together and started grinding together as they danced, just like they used to do in their clubber days. Jonathan was sandwiched between the two muscular men, Dom in front and Ben firmly in behind, as they laughed and danced together. Jonathan squirmed between the two warm muscular bodies, loving the feeling of the firm muscles encasing him, pressing up against his own solid body.

As their sweaty skin slid together, their natural urges soon took over and the dancing took on a more sexual tone with Dom kissing Jonathan on the mouth and Ben licking and kissing the DJ's neck and shoulders.

Jonathan spun around so that he could kiss both the boys at once. The three-way kiss became quite passionate as the bulges in their pants grew to an indecent size.

"Bedroom?" suggested Dom, to which the boys readily agreed. On the way they started undoing their pants and by the time they reached the bed all three were bare-ass naked. They climbed onto the bed and resumed their intense three-way kiss, this time their erect cocks were rubbing up against each other.

Ben moved down to start eating Jonathan's eight inches of cut manhood, stopping to kiss the DJ's pale, solid chest and defined abs along the way. Dom moved around behind Ben and pushed his face into Ben's beautiful round ass, thrusting his tongue inside the tight rosebud.

"You know I've never seen you guys properly fuck," remarked Jonathan after he'd been enjoying Ben's blowjob for a while.

"Well that's a damn shame." Dom said with a mischievous smile when he took a break from rimming his beau. "We should definitely rectify that."

Dom moved back up to his knees, spat on his hand and used it to further lubricate his cock and Ben's hungry hole. Dom's uncut bare cock started sliding into Ben slowly at first, with Dom giving small gentle thrusts to get deeper inside inch by inch. Jonathan had a spectacular view straight down Ben's pale muscular back and over the curve of his round ass watching Dom's cock sliding in and out. Jonathan was thoroughly enjoying the show, as well as the hot mouth that was engulfing his own hard cock.

With one final thrust Dom was pretty much balls-deep, at which point Ben pushed backwards to have his fiancé inside as deep as possible. Ben's muffled moans of delight increased in volume as the pounding of his ass became more and more fierce. Dom leaned forward to kiss Jonathan over the back of his fiancé, who was writhing in pleasure happy that his holes were being put to their good natural use.

Dom picked up the pace as he came closer to blowing, his hips slamming repeatedly into Ben's bubble butt. After a few minutes he could hold his orgasm off no longer and started unloaded his thick white cream directly inside the warm and welcoming passage.

Ben loved the familiar feeling of Dom's cock throbbing inside him as it spread its seed. He stopped sucking on Jonathan and leaned back to kiss Dom deeply before moving forward off of the manly meat and collapsing back on the bed. The other two lay down next to him and they cuddled for a bit, enjoying the warmth of each other's touch.

"So who wants to fuck me?" asked Jonathan

"I'd love to," replied Ben eagerly, quickly slipping off of the bed and fetching the condoms and lube that he had left in the bathroom.

Dom decided to help prepare Jonathan further and give him a good deep rimming while Ben was suiting up. He turned his friend over so that he was face down, his ass in the air and attacked the waiting hole with his expert mouth.

Ben was ready quite quickly but enjoyed watching Dom at work, so he let them continue on for a few minutes before taking his prize. Dom then moved aside and Ben pulled Jonathan back to his knees and eased himself inside. Ben guessed by the tightness of Jonathan's passage that it had been a while so he started off tenderly before working up to longer and faster strokes. He gathered he was doing a good job by the way Jonathan was moaning and muttering "Fuck yeah" as he kept poking inside.

Dom held Ben from behind, whispering in his ear encouraging him to plough Jonathan even harder, which he did.

Jonathan didn't object at all and, if anything, his moans of enjoyment became louder as Ben battered his ass with his thick seven inches. After fifteen minutes of a very good pounding, Jonathan motioned for Ben to pause for a sec.

"Want to make it a double act?"

The duo had no objections and soon Dom was also suited up. They pushed Jonathan flat on the bed and Dom came in behind Ben but slightly lower down so that he could squeeze his cock into Jonathan's already full hole.

The boys moved slowly at first just letting their cocks rub up against each other and stretch out Jonathan's ass. Then they built up into a more forceful rhythm, pumping his ass with more power. The perspiration dripped between the three of them, making them slipperier as the fucking intensified.

Jonathan cried out as the cocks stretched him wider and wider. He felt like they were trying to rip him open and he loved it. Jonathan swore at them and demanded that they fuck him as hard as they could. They built up to a feverish pace and unfortunately weren't able to keep it up as the loads in the boys respective balls were ready to erupt. Dom exploded first, followed swiftly by Ben as he felt Dom's cock throbbing next to his. They were panting like dogs as the cum spurted out into the protective sheaths.

Jonathan loved the pressure of the two men bearing down on him and the throbbing of the cocks inside him. When they were spent they lay there just relaxing for a while as the boys continued to kiss and caress each other, trying to catch their breath after such a brilliant fuck. Eventually the two cocks slid back out of Jonathan's quite sore ass, and they rolled off of him. Jonathan turned over and started wanking to get his much needed release. Ben and Dom went either side of him, holding him in tight, playing with his nipples and balls, giving him gentle kisses along his face and neck. It took less than a minute before he started blowing his load all over himself, his ass contracting with every spurt, giving him a small burst of pain, which reminded him of the recent invasion. When he had finished they lay there for a few minutes before they wearily climbed out of the bed and dragged their sweat-drenched bodies to the bathroom.

After their efforts they were exhausted, so they decided to take advantage of the hotel's limitless hot water. The boys got into the shower and let the hot water rinse them clean. Jonathan suggested they'd be more comfortable sitting on the shower floor, seeing it was big enough for the three of them. Dom sat down first with his back against the wall, and then Ben sat in the inviting space between his legs. Jonathan then sat down facing the boys with his legs overlapping both of theirs. The boys stayed in place, holding each other while the water continued to beat down on them.

After twenty minutes of rest, and letting the water soothe their tired bodies, they decided to hop up and get out before they turned into total prunes. Before they got out, however, Jonathan wanted to thank them for their efforts and give them one last pre-wedding gift, so he sank to his knees and proceeded to alternatively suck the two thick wet cocks in front of him. Ben and Dom continued to kiss as Jonathan treated them to with his skilled mouth, moving from one cockhead to another. The fiancés soon tensed up as they grew close to exploding. Jonathan increased his pace, desperate to taste those delicious loads. He was soon rewarded as the boys spurted their hot cream all over his face and lightly hairy chest, which he lapped up as fast as he could. When they were done they pulled Jonathan to his feet and held him between them as they let the water rinse off the rest of their cum.

They got out of the shower, helped dry each other off and then returned to the bedroom. Jonathan stayed a little longer, lying naked on the bed with the boys, kissing and rolling around, but eventually made moves to leave. He wanted to give the happy couple their privacy and he wanted to be rested and ready for the long day of celebrating ahead of all of them.

When Jonathan went down to the car park he bumped into Andy, whom he'd met a few times before at the café. They chatted for a little bit before hopping into their respective cars. Even though there was a definite attraction between the DJ and *pâtissier* both of them were too tired from their recent exploits to do anything about it. They bid each other goodbye and said that they'd catch up tomorrow at the wedding.

* * *

Finally the big day arrived; and what a stunning day it was. There wasn't a single cloud to spoil the pristine blue sky. It was also in the mid twenties temperature-wise so pleasant for everyone in their more formal attire.

After enjoying a leisurely breakfast together, the Groomal party and those guests staying in the hotel went back to their rooms to get ready before meeting up on the terrace for the pre-wedding cocktail party.

Ben and Dom looked ever so dashing in their charcoal-gray bespoke suits. They both had black ties but had gone for complimentary shirts rather than being completely identical – neither of them being a grand fan of couples dressing the same. Dom wore a bright red shirt with a royal blue handkerchief in his suit pocket and Ben had the inverse. Their best men also looked quite sharp in their matching, fitted black suits with crisp white shirts and black ties. All four of them had blue roses in their lapels; a special order they'd had shipped in from out of state.

Ben and Dom were immaculately coiffed, thanks to the attentions of the hotel hairstylist. Adam's hair was firmly back in his habitual ponytail and Seb's unruly surfer locks had been momentarily tamed by the hair paste Thomas had lent him.

The guests started arriving from around midday and everyone was enjoying the delicious creamy cocktails. Among the crowd was Max, the new counter-hand, who'd come with his boyfriend Pete. Adam and Seb had been tasked with wandering around making sure that none of the guests became too inebriated before the main event. Fortunately, everyone was rather well behaved and when it came time for the ceremony to start at 3pm the congregation was in a happy, if slightly buzzed, mood and all ready to see the boys legally declare their love for each other.

Margaret, their celebrant, gave a most beautiful introduction and welcome to the crowd, which was then followed by various readings from special friends. Dom and Ben then exchanged their own heartfelt vows, with each of them proudly proclaiming exactly how much the other meant to him – by which point there was barely a dry eye in the house. Even the boys' normally stoic fathers were seen to be a little overcome with emotion.

Just before they exchanged their rings – plain platinum bands engraved simply with their initials and date of the wedding – Margaret uttered a twist on the standard phrase "If anyone knows of any reason why these nuptials should not take place, keep it to yourself and the door is that way." A gentle twitter of laughter flowed through the crowd.

When it was quiet again Margaret asked "Do you, Dominique Marinos, take Benjamin Reynolds to be your lawfully wedded husband?"

"I do!" Dom replied with the biggest grin on his face, as he slid the ring on Ben's finger.

Margaret proceeded on with "Do you, Benjamin Reynolds, take Dominique Marinos to be your lawfully wedded husband?"

"Damn straight I do!" he responded, tears forming at the corner of his big brown eyes as he slipped the ring onto Dom's finger.

This in turn made Dom's eyes start to well up with joy as well.

"By the power invested in me by City Hall, I now pronounce you husband and husband! You may now kiss your groom!" exclaimed Margaret, to which they did rather enthusiastically before remembering they were in mixed company and that their relatives may not appreciate such a display.

"May I present Mr and Mr Marinos-Reynolds." announced Margaret to the assembled guests to which there was much clapping and cheers.

The boys turned towards the assembled throng and were instantly showered in a mixture of red and blue rose petals, seemingly coming from everywhere – there were some very enthusiastic throwers in the crowd. Then their friends and family surged forward, seeing that the official part was done, all anxious to bestow their good wishes upon the happy couple.

They accepted the waves of congratulations and posed for a ridiculous amount of photos, which people started posting to their various social media accounts almost straight away – the marvels of modern technology.

A soft breeze was blowing across the terrace, ruffling the decorations and keeping everyone refreshed throughout the festivities. After the ceremony it was back to cocktails and canapés while Ben, Dom and Spencer went off to do some official shots. Everyone was mingling with ease as Jonathan kept the music relaxed and light, leaving the faster and harder mixes for the younger crowd after the dinner.

The boys did manage to escape briefly for a proper wedding kiss in their suite after they'd finished with Spencer but knew that they couldn't get too carried away as they had to get back to their guests and would be missed if their absence was too prolonged. That being said they gave each other a proper groping and had to wait a minute or two before their very noticeable erections had faded away before rejoining the party.

Margaret, who was also acting as MC, guided the crowd to sit down at their respective tables so that the waiters could begin serving. The entrees were brought out just as the sun set over the harbor. The soft twilight was enhanced by paper lanterns, which had been set up over the terrace, so the guests could still see well enough to eat.

Trent and Matt were working the event and gave sneaky grins and winks to their former playmates as they served dinner, not that they weren't equally as attentive to all the other handsome men in attendance.

Ben and Dom were extremely pleased with how everything has worked out. They were also very happy to be feeling the love from all their family and friends and were almost overwhelmed by all the well wishes and messages of support they had received over the evening.

* * *

There had been all manner of speeches during the dinner, mostly funny and sweet. It had helped that they had insisted on a time limit to avoid any long, rambling boring ones. They were about halfway through the proceedings when Spencer noticed his batteries were getting quite low, so right after they'd finished with the mains, he asked a passing waiter, for somewhere to charge up his equipment.

The waiter was Matt, who then took Spencer downstairs one level to a locked storeroom which would be safe enough for Spencer to leave his gear charging without fear of someone taking off with it.

There was an initial spark between the two but Spencer was in professional mode and not about to instigate any naughtiness while he was working. They entered the room, which was only slightly bigger than a broom cupboard and Matt showed him where he could plug in the charger. Spencer could think of better things to be plugged.

Matt turned around quickly and accidentally bumped up against Spencer – he was a bit of klutz of late. Matt instantly apologized but then they stood there, pressed up against each other, not saying a word for almost a minute before Matt decided to take the initiate and dived in for a kiss. Spencer didn't hesitate in kissing the naughty boy back. They furiously made out, pulling at each other's clothes. Spencer's suit and Matt's work pants and shirt becoming quite undone. They knew that they had to be relatively quick, seeing as they both had work to do and would be in grave trouble if they got caught fooling around.

Spencer in particular didn't want to miss any important shots but he knew he had about thirty minutes or so before the wedding cake would be brought out, giving him a little leeway.

Matt swiftly dropped to his knees, whipped down Spencer's pants and started sucking on the gorgeous big dick he'd just released, teasing the foreskin with his tongue before swallowing the shaft down his greedy throat. Conscious of the time, he then quickly moved lower to play with the big smooth balls and between Spencer's legs, his tongue reaching under and into the crease of the ass.

Spencer pulled him up and they kissed some more before Spencer went down to reciprocate Matt's fine work. He did a superb job, running his hands over Matt's ripped torso and up to tweak his small dark-brown nipples, as he ably deep-throated the waiter's stiff cock.

Matt enjoyed Spencer's practiced attentions and it wasn't long before his load built up to point of needing a quick escape. He warned Spencer that he was going to blow but Spencer kept working the shaft, sucking and worshipping it with his tongue. The first shot went straight to the back of Spencer's throat, so then he pulled back and let the rest spurt and smear over his face. It was at this point that the door suddenly opened, both boys having neglected to lock it in their rush to play, and in walked Trent.

Quickly assessing the situation he locked the door behind himself, walked towards them, bent over and licked his co-worker's cum straight off of Spencer's face.

Trent then stood up and gave Matt a hearty kiss. Spencer, always adaptable, soon was undoing Trent's pants, eager to have another load splattered on his skin. Matt and Trent continued kissing with their pants around their ankles, while Spencer applied his talented tongue and warm mouth to Trent's meat, all the while keeping a hand on Matt's cock, coaxing it back to life.

Once Spencer successfully got both boys erect – not a particularly difficult feat – he wanted to join the boys on their feet so he climbed up slowly, kissing and licking his way up the two boys, alternating between Matt's lean twinkish build and Trent's more solid muscular frame. When he made it to the top he pushed his way into a steamy three-way kiss – not that they seemed to object at all. The trio kept making out for a few more minutes, their half naked bodies rubbing up against each other in a frantic fashion.

Trent wanted to make the most of their brief time together, so he moved to the ground and got behind

Spencer. He grabbed the tanned round ass cheeks and spread them wide open. He eased his big hands forward so that his fingers could start to fiddle with the sensitive hole in the middle. After he had opened up the entrance a little, he thrust his tongue into the hole and gave Spence a nice deep rimming. Trent wanted to fuck this plump ass no matter how short a time they had.

After looking down and seeing what Trent was up to Matt got back on his knees and started blowing Spencer once more. The photographer was left writhing between the two hungry mouths that were voraciously devouring him.

Happily, Trent had refilled his pockets since yesterday and had protection ready and raring to go. As Trent undid the packet and rolled on the condom, he kept his face firmly wedged in between the tanned globes of Spencer's magnificent ass. When he was ready he stood up, put his cockhead at the saliva-soaked entrance and pushed gently inside.

Spencer was a little surprised at first but quickly relaxed and ground his ass backwards into Trent's crotch. Soon he had the entire seven inches of the wonderfully thick dick in to the hilt and could feel Trent's trimmed pubes brushing against the smooth skin of his buttocks.

Trent started pumping straight away, refilling Spencer's hospitable hole with each manly stroke. Each thrust also pushed Spencer's cock further down Matt's throat; he was still on his knees worshipping the fine, uncut cock. Trent started to really slam into Spencer, desperate to give the photographer a ride to remember.

It only took about five minutes of such rough cocking before Spencer couldn't help but unload down Matt's keen throat.

Matt drank it all down like the good little cocksucker he was, happy to have a belly full of cum.

After a few more strokes, coupled with the contractions of Spencer's ass around his cock, Trent easily filled the condom with his seed.

The boys then offered to help finish Matt off but he didn't want to go again, choosing to wait till after his shift was over to get his second round off. They used a box of paper napkins that were in the storeroom to wipe each other down, before reclothing themselves and venturing back out to the party and their jobs.

* * *

Fortunately for Spencer, he arrived back on the terrace with plenty of time to spare before the arrival of the wedding cake and his absence hadn't been remarked upon by anybody in attendance. He was, however, accosted almost immediately by Dom's mother, who had recently had a meeting with him about doing some freelance work for her upcoming agency. Neither of them had realized at the time the connection they already shared…small, small world. They chatted briefly before Spencer excused himself, as he had more wedding shots to get.

Not long afterwards, the cake arrived, brought in by Trent and Matt, to the excited 'oohs' and 'ahs' of the crowd. It was widely known that Dom had made it himself and his reputation for mouth-watering creations had them eager for a taste. Indeed, after it had been cut and served, there seemed to be a general consensus amongst the guests as to the remarkable deliciousness of the honey fruitcake and the vanilla icing.

Andy was rather relieved that Dom hadn't appeared to notice the repair job he had been forced to do the previous night. Apparently, his faith in his culinary skills was well justified.

After everyone had had their cake, they were all handed and a glass of champagne, and Seb proposed a toast to the happy couple.

"To two of the most beautiful, loving men I've ever known; may you continue to make each other as happy as your love makes us." This was followed by many a 'hear hear' and occasional clap.

The waiters then placed out trays of cupcakes – Blue Velvet and Peanut Butter with white chocolate – to tempt anyone who still had room for more treats.

Frankly, with everything that had been served it was a wonder they hadn't already succumbed to food comas. They continued to eat their cupcakes and drink champagne, chatting amongst themselves, for about twenty minutes, until Margaret, announced that it was time to take to the dance floor for the first official dance of the newlyweds.

Dom and Ben took to the floor and slow danced to the song that had been playing on their portable radio at the secluded beach when they had first said their "I love yous". They didn't share the fact that it had been after a particularly vigorous fuck and that they had been covered in each other's cum at the time.

Everyone was starting to get rather buzzed by this point and the dancing began in earnest, with all the couples taking to the floor. Jonathan did his best to keep the crowd entertained, in between checking out the talent on the dance floor. Jonathan had caught many an eye that night, and he certainly intended making at least one of their acquaintances when the opportunity arose later that evening.

Not that he had ever really struggled to find male companionship at the end of the night if he wanted it but he had noticed that the higher his DJ profile the hotter and easier the guys seemed to become.

* * *

After the cake cutting Dimitri and Jay snuck off to the bathrooms two levels below for a quick play, knowing they would be less likely to be interrupted. One thing led to another and what had started out as a cheeky bit of head escalated to Dimitri shoving his thick cock deep inside Jay's accommodating ass. They were fucking rather noisily in a toilet cubicle when interrupted by a voice outside the door claiming to be security.

"Excuse me gentlemen but we've had some complaints about indecent behavior. Could you open the door please?" said more as statement by a deep booming voice. Dimitri reluctantly pulled out of Jay's warm passage and they embarrassedly opened the door. Where they saw it was Eric.

"You fucker!" yelled Dimitri, punching Eric in the arm for interrupting a perfectly good fuck. Dimitri's irritation quickly faded and he dragged Eric into the cubicle with them. Eric had been an early crush of Dimitri's, and had fantasized about him a good many times after Dom had brought him home for dinner the first time. Now that enough time had passed Dimitri decided that Eric was now fair game and wanted to make some of those fantasies come true.

Dimitri pressed Eric up against the wall and kissed him hard, while undoing the buttons of his shirt so he could rub his hands over the newcomer's waxed solid chest.

Jay decided to help things along by ripping at Eric's belt to get his pants off and expose the thick cock concealed inside. The tandem effort worked well and Eric was soon standing before them fully showing off his manly, sculpted build. Jay handed Eric a condom, then bent over the toilet, as he had been when he had Dimitri inside of him, and offered his ass up for pounding – an offer rarely refused.

Eric eagerly agreed, rolled on the condom and aimed his loaded weapon for the target. He slid in easily – seeing Jay had been full of Dimitri only a few minutes beforehand – and started pumping away. Dimitri got to his knees and spread Eric's ass and started fingering him as he violated Jay's ass.

"Fuck me harder bitch!" demanded Jay, who was keen to have his hole get a proper work out.

Not wanting to disappoint, Eric started forcefully driving his eight inches into Jay's obliging orifice. He was instantly rewarded by the lustful sounds of approval from the stunning Eurasian man before him.

Unseen by Eric, Dimitri had also slipped on a condom. Before Eric knew what was happening Dimitri had popped his cockhead inside Eric's hairy hole and slammed himself inside all the way to base. Eric attempted to yell but Dimitri silenced him with a hand over his mouth.

Dimitri waited a minute for Eric to adjust and let the older man set his own rhythm sliding in and out of Jay's hole as Dimitri's meat did the same to him.

Eric relished being sandwiched between the two young lovers. Eric took it as well as he gave but all the stimulation of his prostate and the feel of Jay's silky smooth passage had him blowing after only a few minutes.

"Weak!" teased Dimitri. At which point Eric hopped off of Dimitri's cock and reached his hand back and slapped the side of Dimitri's ass. He took off his cum filled condom and threw it in the bin at the side and was preparing to pull up his pants to leave.

"Not so fast." said Dimitri, as he stopped Eric from putting his pants back on.

"I think he needs to be punished." Jay said to Dimitri who rapidly agreed. Jay quickly grabbed another condom from his suit pants pocket and rolled it on.

"Sit on him." commanded Dimitri.

Eric made a few half-hearted protests then did as he was told. He straddled Jay, who was now sitting on the toilet seat, and dutifully began to impale himself on the ten solid inches beneath him. Eric leaned forward and kissed Jay slowly, their tongues circling each other, while his ass stretched to accommodate the intruder. Having had Dimitri just inside him helped a lot and soon he found he felt Jay's trimmed black pubes grazing his ass cheeks. Eric stayed in Jay's lap, squirming, letting the cock settle and open him up wide before he felt ready to start moving up and down on it. It wasn't the biggest he'd ever had but it was definitely up there.

Dimitri was still hard and hadn't removed his condom. He let Eric bounce up and down getting used to the massive meat inside him before he moved in closer.

Jay guessed what he was up to and swiftly grabbed Eric's hips and pulled him up so that he only had an inch of cock still inside him. Dimitri put his condom-covered cock up against Jay's and little by little forced his way into Eric's, already quite full, passage.

Eric, who'd also had quite a bit to drink, was more relaxed than normal and didn't really protest as the boys began to open him up even further. He did begin to make a lot of noise so Jay started kissing again him to help muffle the moans, lest they attract the attention of the real security.

Eric was in heaven with all that cock stuffed inside him, rubbing up against each other, stretching his sphincter and battering his prostate. His hole hadn't been worked like this since a bout of fisting about a year ago…they certainly weren't small boys.

Jay and Dimitri repeatedly rammed their cocks inside the tender passage, not taking any heed of Eric's pleas of mercy. They kept ploughing away until their balls were ready for final release. Jay went first as he ably filled his condom with a hefty amount of seed.

Seeing the pleasure in his Jay's eyes and feeling the throbbing of the cock next to his drove Dimitri to the brink; so he roughly pulled out of Eric's battered ass, tore off his condom and wanked for all of five seconds before blowing his load all over Eric's bare ass. His hot load ran down over the round muscular cheeks and dripped all over Jay's balls, who was still jammed deep inside Eric.

Jay then slowly pulled out, gave Eric one more kiss and a hard slap on his well-serviced ass. Eric stood up unsteadily and leaned on Dimitri for support until he got back the proper use of his legs. The three cleaned themselves up with the toilet paper and soon had wiped away all visible traces of their adventures. Although, internally Eric knew he would be feeling that fuck for more than a few days. They pulled up their pants, buttoned up their shirts and generally rearranged themselves as best they could in their inebriated condition and headed back out to the reception.

* * *

Ben was dancing with Dom and noticed Dimitri and Jay coming back in a bit disheveled, he caught Dimitri's eye and just shook his head smiling. Dimitri only gave a proud grin in response. The dancing had been going for

quite a while by this point and the older invitees and those who had brought their children – mostly the nieces and nephews of Ben and Dom – had long since departed to the comfort of their beds.

The younger guests, mostly comprising of gay men, were still partying up a storm, as they knew they had use of the terrace until four in the morning and were intent on dancing till the very last minute.

As the party started to wind down Seb was inviting select members of the crowd for a private after-party to be held in his and Thomas' hotel room. Among those he asked was the sexy DJ, who accepted without a second thought. Jonathan had known Seb for quite a while and knew exactly what sort of shenanigans would be in store.

Seb had also asked Trent and Matt as they had been clearing away the remaining stray plates and glasses that littered the terrace. Again not a great deal of convincing was needed to persuade the boys to attend. Fortunately, both of them had the following day off so had nothing stopping them from enjoying themselves fully.

The last two gentlemen to be invited were Max and Pete after Seb accidentally burst in on them, in the stairwell engaging in a spot of fellatio. They were more than a little embarrassed as they desperately tried to cover up…Max more so, as he had to work with Seb, but he was quickly able to see the funny side of it. Besides he'd already caught Adam and Seb in a similar position in the basement, not long after he'd started at the café. Max also had a fair idea of what the after-party might entail and even though he and Pete were fairly monogamous they weren't opposed to the odd bit of extramarital activity when the situation arose.

Finally, Jonathan was forced to switch off his music but not before leaving the crowd with a phenomenal mash-up of Kylie, Gaga and Katy Perry, which had the remaining few souls cheering and dancing about with gay abandon. Ben and Dom had already retired to their honeymoon suite a few hours earlier, apparently keen to fulfil their husbandly duties as soon as possible.

The small group that was left bid each other farewell and headed downstairs for taxis and such, while those lucky enough to be invited to Seb's special soirée made their way to his suite on the 15th floor.

* * *

Seb was well organized, as usual when it came to matters of sex, and had the suite prepared for a most memorable party. In the corner he had a duffle bag full of condoms and bottles of lube, which he planned on distributing later. He didn't want there to be anything to hamper their fun, especially something as frustrating as a lack of suitable supplies. He had also relied on Adam to get a hold of a whole trolley load of towels, sheets and cleaning products beforehand. Seb thought it only fair to clean up any excess mess themselves, as they didn't want to scar the poor cleaning staff for life.

For nourishment, Seb had grabbed a few boxes of leftover cupcakes and had also managed to snag a small crate of champagne – Ben and Dom had bought a vast quantity to avoid the terrible proposition of running out. Seb figured the boys would need to replenish their energy once the party games started.

The atmosphere became more and more jovial, if slightly drunken, as the number of men increased. By about half past four in the morning everyone had arrived. All in all there were fifteen men in attendance, including all the staff from the café and their partners, the two waiters and the DJ. They were spread throughout the suite chatting in small groups, some were dancing, some were kissing and some were starting to become even more intimate.

Thomas, Dimitri, Jay and Seb had resumed their hot foursome, commandeering the king-size bed. They recreated the pose from the day before but this time it was Seb defiling Jay, who was on his hands and knees locked in a fervent sixty-nine with Thomas. Thomas was lying contentedly on his back while Dimitri pounded his passage with Seb and Dimitri occasionally leaning forward to kiss over the two lusty lads between them.

Outside on the small balcony, Spencer and James had been chatting together, seated side by side, overlooking the city lights. As they spoke they drew closer and closer together, their legs brushing up against each other. After a little while Spencer couldn't help himself and just had to taste James' lips and leaned forward for a soft, gentle kiss.

James had his hand resting on Spencer's thigh which moved higher up as they kissed. He'd wanted to do this ever since he first saw Spencer with his camera at the wedding. Their kissing became more passionate, as they pulled at each other's clothing, quickly discarding shirts, pants, underwear and socks. They had completely forgotten about everyone that could see them through the glass doors back to the lounge room. Although, this wasn't a problem seeing that everyone there was already engaged in the same sort of behavior.

Andy and Jonathan were naked on the lounge together. The mutual attraction from the night before was finally given a chance to spark. They had started off kissing, their naked bodies rubbing up against each other, the black and white contrast of skin colors making for a very erotic sight.

Jonathan loved the taste of Andy, and licked him all over from his lips, to his nipples, juicy cock and big black bubble butt. He loved the musky scent in his nostrils as he pushed his face deeper inside. Once he'd given Andy a decent rimming, Jonathan whipped on a condom. Then he bent the *pâtissier* over the side of the lounge, spread Andy's cheeks wide and shoved his cock deep inside the waiting hole.

Jonathan wasn't gentle, fucking Andy hard as he kept a tight grip on his firm black hips. After a little while, Jonathan pulled out and laid on his back on the lounge and motioned for Andy to ride him.

Andy eagerly complied; he squatted over the DJ's thick eight inches and soon his round buttocks were bouncing off Jonathan's thrusting hips. They went on to change positions a few more times as Jonathan wanted to poke and prod every last inch of Andy's amazing ass. After a while they flip-flopped and Andy forced his big black meat deep inside the DJ's willing ass.

Meanwhile, just in front of them on the Oriental rug, Adam, Steve and Matt were happily fucking away on the floor. Steve was hammering away at the waiter's spectacular little toned ass, while Adam fucked Matt's face. Steve had his hand pressed down on Matt's lower back, covering the tattoo beneath. Matt liked the pressure of Steve's hand pushing him down as the solid cock invaded him.

After an exhaustive fucking Steve pulled out and sat back, and beckoned Adam to come down on the floor next to him. Adam grabbed a condom and smiled while he suited up, as he had guessed what his boyfriend wanted to do. Steve and Adam slid right together so that their cocks were pressed up against one another.

Matt took the hint and lowered himself down, stopping just as the heads were pushing against his entrance. Matt wanted to take his time adjusting before the assault of two cocks into his tender hole began fully. He slowly welcomed them inside, as they pushed and poked, until they were both deeply embedded in his incredibly tight passage. As Matt moved himself up and down the shafts, sweat ran down his body and dripped onto the hot couple fucking him. The twink was in absolute ecstasy, as the cocks inside him moved rhythmically and stretched his ass like never before – this was his first time being double penetrated, after all. Although, given his guttural moans of pleasure, it was unlikely to be the last.

In the bathroom, Max and Pete had joined Eric and Trent in the hot tub. Both couples were making out, as the hot bubbling water caressed their naked bodies. Due to the hot tub's size their four bodies kept bumping and rubbing together. While they were still focused on their separate couplings, stray hands still found themselves wandering amongst the four of them.

Max was sitting in Pete's lap facing into his hazel eyes as they kissed, he could feel Pete's eight inches of uncut goodness rubbing against his ass, searching for the entrance. Max shifted slightly so Pete's cock could slide between his cheeks and find his hairy hole. The oily water acted as a lubricant but it was still a rough entry as the intruder hit its intended target and pushed inside Max. Pete ran his hand through Max's dark, wavy hair as he gently thrust upwards, holding on tightly to his boyfriend's solid, stocky frame. Max adored the feeling of his boyfriend's bare cock exploring his insides and pleasuring his prostate.

Next to them, Trent and Eric were at a similar point. Eric preferred to top, given the battering his ass had taken earlier from Jay and Dimitri, so they both stood up in the tub. Trent then bent over the side of the hot tub, bracing himself on the railing. Eric grabbed a condom from the pile on the shelf next to them and prepared himself for action. Once wrapped, Eric slammed into Trent's ass and started pounding the tight ass straight away, he watched Trent's muscular back contracting as he wriggled on the hard cock.

Trent took Eric's thick cock with glee, enjoying each thrust, the warm water splashing around them and tickling his balls while his cock was pressed up against the side of the hot tub. He really enjoyed being roughly fucked, especially by older, more hairy, muscular men…Like Steve and Eric. Trent could feel Eric's tough hands holding his hips tight, pulling him back to be impaled even deeper by the rigid cock.

By this time Spencer and James had moved inside and were now on the bed next to the foursome of Seb, Dimitri, Jay and Thomas – who were still going strong in their endeavors. Spencer was on his back being ploughed relentlessly by James. He could feel James' smooth balls banging against the top of his ass, as the thick uncut monster raided his hole.

James gazed deeply into Spencer's bright blue eyes as he pounded away, kissing him and feeling the heat of their connection. He had already decided that this wouldn't be the last time, their sexual chemistry merited more than just a one-off fuck. James had a feeling that Spencer would be amenable to more play, especially after he felt the photographer's nails raking down his back when he started to really pound hard.

The foursome on the bed next to them gradually started to swallow them up. James felt a latex-covered cock knocking at his entrance; he turned his head and saw it was Dimitri so he graciously granted entry. Thomas and Jay then put their cocks in between James and Spencer so they kissed with the two pieces of meat in front of them.

At this point Seb went out of the bedroom to see what all the other guys were up to. He came across Adam and Steve double-fucking Matt who was leaning forward to kiss Jonathan, who in turn was being ploughed from behind by Andy. After watching for a little while he went into the bathroom and saw that Eric was fucking Pete against the side of the hot tub while Trent was slamming his cock into Matt's plump ass…the boys having swapped their couplings about five minutes earlier. Hesitant to disturb the boys he quickly mentioned to them that there was more fun to be had in the bedroom when they were ready. They continued fucking for a few more minutes before following after the sexy, bronzed counter-hand.

Seb had also given the same message to the boys in the lounge room, as he collected a platter of cupcakes and rejoined the others. Bit by bit they were drawn into the bedroom. Matt, Steve and Adam came in and hopped on the bed taking whatever holes and cocks they could see free, then in came Jonathan and Andy followed soon after by the boys from the bathroom.

To help move things along Seb then encouraged the others to make use of the cupcakes. Seb demonstrated by grabbing two and smashing them on Dimitri's hairy legs and ass, and then ravenously eating them all up. The other boys soon got into the spirit of the occasion and squished the tasty treats all over each other – cream and cake crumbs going everywhere. It was a scene of utter chaos and decadence and every single one of them knew it was night they'd never forget.

They sucked and licked away, pleasuring each other's bodies – playing with anything they could get their hands on…or in. The condom supplies were decimated as they kept swapping partners like they were playing some sort of slutty version of musical chairs.

All the boys were in awe of Jay's meat – at ten inches he was the biggest amongst them and everyone was keen to have a ride. Jay was more than happy to oblige and impale as many of their snug asses as he could.

By the end of the party, they had drenched the bedroom in their sweat and cum – the scent of sex heavy in the air. The remnants of their man-on-man loving were also strewn throughout the suite with most furniture now having a sticky surface. Indeed, you could have filled a sperm bank to bursting with all the seed splashed about the place.

Once all their balls were well and truly drained, they took turns showering, going in groups of twos and threes – to save water of course – until all of them were as clean as dirty boys could ever get. They slowly organized themselves as to who would graciously share their hotel rooms with those who hadn't taken a room. By this time it was quite light outside and they didn't want to force anyone to face the indignity of a cab ride home, especially if there was chance for more fucking when they awoke from their slumber.

Adam and Steve took Eric, Trent and Matt back with them. They let the two waiters crash on the big comfy lounge, while they invited Eric in to sleep with them. Adam treasured having Steve and Eric either side of him, wrapping him in a beautifully warm and cosy cocoon of man muscle.

James took Spencer, Jonathan and Andy back to his spacious room. Jonathan and Andy volunteered to take the couch together, as they wanted a bit more alone time together. They actually stayed up for a few more hours quietly chatting while wrapped up in each other's arms.

This worked out just fine for James who invited Spencer in to cuddle with him. The two fell asleep quite quickly, with James holding Spencer from behind, his resting cock pressed into the comfy cushion of Spencer's soft, round ass.

Dimitri and Jay hadn't booked a room so Seb and Thomas happily welcomed them back into their bed. The foursome had grown quite close over the weekend's festivities and had made plans to spend more time together in the coming week. Max and Pete were also without lodgings so they were given the couch. They decided to deal with the clean-up tomorrow only bothering to change the sheets in the bedroom and cover the lounge with towels given the number of fresh wet stains on it.

As they drifted off to sleep, the boys thanked Seb for all his hard work and Seb fell asleep with a huge smirk on his beautiful face.

* * *

A few hours earlier, up at the door of the honeymoon suite, Ben and Dom had finally escaped their loving group of well wishers and had some desperately needed time alone. When they opened the door Ben suddenly picked up Dom by the waist, hoisted him over his shoulder and carried him across the threshold. They only managed a few paces, due to them laughing like maniacs, before collapsing onto the nearby lounge.

Dom had organized for his little fairy helpers – Seb and Adam – to cover the bed in hundreds of red rose petals with the trail leading from the front door. The lights were set to a low soothing intensity and there were tea light candles along the base of the balcony.

The best men had stocked the mini bar full of chilled champagne, strawberries and chocolates. The boys had also left a surprise on the counter – two fresh seed cakes – with contributions from rest of the café staff. Dom and

Ben happily gobbled them down, rather enjoying the salty almost-caramel aftertaste.

Ben and Dom had deliberately paced themselves with the food and drink throughout the festivities, so they would be in the small minority of couples that manage to consummate their marriage on the actual wedding night.

They stripped off their wedding suits and were soon naked rolling around together on the floor by the lounge. Dom reached up for the champagne bottle on the counter nearby and prepared to open it. Ben's eyes widened as he thought Dom wanted to fill his ass with champagne, as payback for what he had done to him when they'd become engaged.

Truthfully, Dom had thought about it but had another idea in mind. He shook the bottle for a few seconds before he popped the cork and sprayed Ben's face, chest and crotch. Dom then turned the bottle on himself, the bubbly alcoholic liquid dripping all over their beautifully defined bodies. Dom moved down and pinned Ben against the floor as he kissed him with ardor.

They continued to roll around on the floor together, their hands slipping and sliding over each other's sticky wet skin. Dom moved down and took Ben's magnificent manhood in his mouth, teasing the shaft with his tongue and light touches of his teeth. Ben wrapped his solid thighs around Dom's head, locking it in place.

Dom was happy to be trapped, his nose buried in Ben's brown pubes and his chin rubbing up against his new husband's heavy balls. He took Ben's cock deep in his throat, milking it with his mouth. Dom stayed there working Ben's crotch for a good ten minutes before standing up, then helping Ben to his feet. Dom pushed Ben up against the window, with the splendid night view over the twinkling lights of the harbor. Dom then squatted down, spread Ben's luscious ass and thrust his tongue inside the exposed hole.

Ben pushed back, as was only natural, and let Dom's mouth work its magic on his hungry hole. All the stimulation by Dom's tongue and fingers was almost more than he could bear.

"I want you in me!" he demanded and Dom swiftly obliged.

Ben was in absolute heaven as he felt Dom's balls slapping hard against his butt with each powerful thrust. He was so happy to be finally married to the man he loved and to be fucked so skillfully to boot.

Dom loved watching Ben's body tense up and relax, as he pounded into the perfectly padded ass. Dom pressed into Ben, his hands on top of his husband's, both splayed against the glass. He ground his bare cock in a circular motion, really driving deep into Ben's passage.

After a little while they decided it'd be fun to fuck on their big balcony over the railing. Dom double-checked that it was sturdy, as he had no intention of flying over the edge on their special night and ending up as a novelty piece of trash news.

Dom took his position, bent over the railing, his ass exposed and ready for Ben's cock. Ben wasn't slow in taking him up and his offer and was soon balls-deep in Dom's athletic ass. They fucked loudly, grunting, cursing and moaning, but given how high up they were and the double glazed hotel windows they doubted anyone would hear them and they were right. The windows were so good they couldn't hear a thing from the orgy going on in the room directly beneath them, although it wouldn't have surprised either of them to find out what Seb had orchestrated.

Despite their strenuous efforts, the balcony proved too chilly after a while, so they moved back inside and proceeded to desecrate the honeymoon suite properly. They fucked up against the walls, over the back of the lounge, on the bathroom floor – and pretty much every surface in between. They finished up back in their bed for the grand finale – neither of them having yet cum.

Dom was on his hands and knees being taken roughly from behind by Ben. His husband pummeled his ass repeatedly, their sweaty bodies slamming together. Ben slapped the side of Dom's butt, to punctuate more violent thrusts. Ben could feel that he was close, so pumped Dom harder and faster until his load could be contained no more.

As Dom felt the load gushing in his ass he couldn't hold back his own ejaculation and he soon blew all over the soft sheets. Ben collapsed down on top of Dom, leaving his softening cock wedged inside. Neither of them had ever been happier.

The newlyweds kept dozing and playing, dozing and playing, until the sun's morning light crept into their room bringing with it the new day. As they slowly slipped into slumber their thoughts were of each other and of the many adventures yet to come…like a steamy sex-filled honeymoon.

FRENCH RAISIN TOAST

Ingredients:

2 eggs

2 cups milk

1 teaspoon nutmeg

1 large loaf of unsliced raisin bread

Butter or Olive oil

Instructions:

Mix together the eggs, milk and nutmeg in a large bowl.

Grease a large frying pan with the butter or oil.

Put it on a hotplate at medium heat.

Take the loaf and cut it into thick slices (3cm/1inch).

Soak the slices in the milky mixture until thoroughly coated.

Cook slices in the frying pan until each side is golden brown.

Serve with your choice of accompaniments (strawberries, whipped, cream, maple syrup, bacon…).

HONEY FRUIT CAKE

Ingredients:

3 eggs
1 & 1/4 cups self-raising flour
1 cup fine sugar
1 cup unsalted butter
2 &1/2 cups mixed chopped dried fruit (cherries, raisins, sultanas, pineapple, currants…)
1/2 teaspoon mixed spices
1/2 teaspoon baking soda
1/3 cup liquid honey
1 cup cold water

Instructions:

Preheat oven to 180°C (350°F).

Add the sugar, butter, dried fruit, honey and water to a large saucepan and bring to the boil.

Take it away from the heat, stir it well, cover it with plastic wrap and leave to cool.

Line a square baking tray while mixture is cooling.

Once cool, stir in the eggs, then the flour, baking soda and mixed spices.

Mix well.

Evenly pour mixture into tray and bake for 30-40 minutes.

When cooked, take it out and leave it to cool on the counter.

Decorate as desired.

PEANUT BUTTER CUPCAKES
WITH WHITE CHOCOLATE ICING

Ingredients:

Cupcakes

3 eggs

2 & 1/2 cups flour

1 cup brown sugar

1 cup smooth peanut butter

1 teaspoon baking soda

1 teaspoon lemon juice

1/4 teaspoon salt

1/2 cup unsalted butter

1/2 cup milk

1 teaspoon vanilla extract

Icing

1 cup white chocolate

1 1/3 cup unsalted butter

3/4 cup icing sugar

Instructions:

Preheat oven to 180°C (350°F).

Line cupcake tray with paper liners or use a silicon cupcake mould.

Mix together the butter, peanut butter and brown sugar with an electric mixer until it becomes a fluffy mixture. Add the eggs and vanilla essence to the mixture and beat by hand.

Once combined, add the flour, salt, milk, lemon juice and baking powder and stir well.

Pour mixture evenly into the tray or mould, only filling until 2/3 full.

Bake in the oven for 25 minutes. To test if they are cooked, insert a toothpick in the center and if it comes out clean then they are ready.

While cupcakes are cooking, melt the chocolate in a glass bowl over a saucepan of boiling water.

Combine the butter and icing sugar into a bowl. Best to use an electric mixer for faster results.

When the chocolate has nearly melted take it away from the heat and stir until it has fully melted.

Add the chocolate to the butter and icing sugar, mix well.

Take the cupcakes out of the oven and leave to cool before decorating with the icing.

Lydian Press

ABOUT THE AUTHOR

Jimi could be considered to be something of a refined blend of Australian/Polish heritage – given his passion for the arts, vodka and BBQs. He now lives in Paris with his wonderfully understanding French husband and cats.

For other of his raunchy ramblings and published work, feel free to browse http://www.jimify.me follow him @jimifyme on Twitter & Instagram or show your devotion at facebook.com/JIMIFY.ME

Lydian Press is dedicated to bringing you the finest GLBTQ erotic literature on the web.

Visit us on the web at:

http://lydianpress.com